Happy Birthday

B.

The Found Battleship

Rejtő Jenő

2020.

Translated from Hungarian by Henrietta Whitlock

Original Hungarian Title: A megkerült cirkáló

Copyright © English translation Henrietta Whitlock, 2015

All rights reserved

Contents

Chapter One 5

Chapter Two 11

Chapter Three 16

Chapter Four 22

Chapter Five 31

Chapter Six 37

Chapter Seven 43

Chapter Eight 51

Chapter Nine 59

Chapter Ten 67

Chapter Eleven 85

Chapter Twelve 89

Chapter Thirteen 96

Chapter Fourteen 107

Chapter Fifteen 111

Chapter Sixteen 118

Chapter Seventeen 129

Chapter Eighteen 131

Chapter Nineteen 134

Chapter Twenty 138

Chapter Twenty One 142

Chapter Twenty Two 147

Chapter One

"Your money or your life!"

"My life!"

The armed assailant was so alarmed by this answer that he took a step back. Since the beginning of time, this was the first occasion the above response had been given to this well-known demand. The attacker's revolver, ready to be fired, shook in his hand and he simply did not know what to do. The victim raised both his arms calmly, as if he did not care what happened to him.

In terms of its course and its conclusion, this was the strangest and saddest criminal comedy of all time.

Scene: San Francisco, Oakland.

Written by: life.

Characters:

A nervous bandit.

A resigned victim.

(Military, sparse population.)

Time: money.

"Moron!", repeated the robber. "Your money or your life! Did you not hear me?"

"What are you shouting for? Do you think that I'm deaf? Since I was permitted to choose between giving you my money or my life, I chose my life."

The robber's situation was desperate.

"You'll come to grief if you're making fun of me here! I'll count to three!..."

"You're a maths teacher, I swear! ... I said that you could have my life. I'm a sponger, so I have no bills to pay. But where will I get another fifty cents from if I give it to you?"

Now consider the robber's position. Should he shoot this man, and risk the electric chair for fifty cents, or should he leave in shame following this short conversation?

"I'm warning you for the last time, and then...", he started in a serious tone again.

"Don't give me threats! You gave me a choice, so now please shoot!...", and because he felt pity for the robber waving his revolver clumsily, he added gently: "Put the idea out of your head, dear Mr Marauder, that I will give you a penny. There's no chance of that, believe me, my dear..."

"I'm warning you for the last time: if you're making fun of me here, I'll shoot you like a dog!"

"All right! But hurry up, I don't have time to stand around here all day!...", and he added sniggering with an unarticulated screech, nodding: "You are a great victim in my opinion, Mr robber! A barely corrupted marauder! One like you should not kill a man over fifty cents!... He shouldn't do it for under two dollars. Old Wagner is a great judge of human nature, well, my fine gangster!"...

At this moment, unexpectedly, two soldiers appeared walking by, a few feet away from them.

They would capture him!

The robber shoved his revolver in his pocket, frightened. The victim lowered his arms with a mechanical compliance, turned towards the soldiers and...

He said nothing!

On top of that a rustling was heard above them! Two cycling policemen were pedalling along the embankment, and the victim did not move. The soldiers and policemen moved along. The robber pulled his revolver out with lightning speed and shouted at the victim:

"Not a move, or…"

The other looked around in alarm, and almost crying, but still firmly, said to him:

"Don't shout, you moron! You'll draw all the gendarmes over here… I've never seen such a nervous robber in my life! You're going to cause a lot of inconvenience to me!"

The robber was scared.

Good God! What's this?!

The victim was more afraid of the gendarmes than an armed robber. Who could this man be? What sort of terrible, long wanted criminal?

"Hands up!"

The victim raised his arms angrily.

"Tell me, are you running an exercise class here?!… Upon my word, I've never seen anything like this! It's your mania, with the hands. And thirdly: don't wave that gun about, it may go off and the policemen will come back… I've never seen such a nervous robber!", he whined impatiently, and he had such a large hiccup that his torn top hat sank onto his nose.

"Tell me, are you crazy?"

"Perhaps, but that's not important right now… Listen here, Mr robbevich", the attacked man started diplomatically, to make peace, "give me one dollar and I will let you go. Well?… what are we arguing about here for so long. Right?"

"You'll let me go?", said the marauder in amazement. "You should consider yourself lucky if I just left and didn't hurt you."

"This is also a point of view, but not mine. Hic!... Why are you trembling like that, pal, I only hiccupped... My point of view is different. When you leave, I will simply pull out my knife and smoothly throw it into the back of your neck from behind." And he screeched with a croaky, jovial laugh: "Well, my dear killer! Old Mr Wagner could be an Olympic champion in knife throwing... And just like my one dollar tariff, I will remove my knife from you in record time. You see, this is a good point of view. Well?... you can choose: your money or your life?!"

The marauder completely lost his ground at this. Should he shoot this monster for fifty cents? Or should he risk a knife being thrown into his back when he left? He would become the laughing stock of the world if he paid his victim one dollar, with a revolver in his hand.

The victim was waiting calmly, although a bit unsteadily. He was unbelievably ragged. Even a scarecrow would not have put on his clothes. He did not wear a shirt at all; on the other hand he had tied an old rag around his neck, signalling the importance of this piece of underwear. It could have been a particular sign of identification on wanted notices that a barely wilted gardenia decorated his buttonhole.

The wilted flower was a signal of his unfading childish optimism. It was the symbol of that light, keen spirit, naïve life-philosophy, and ceaseless intoxicating joviality, with which Mr Wagner opened his inner being to the smallest, simplest pleasures in the world, every minute of the day.

His wrinkled, warty, toothless, wide-mouthed, ancient face was framed by a sparse, but long-haired sailor's beard, along his jawbone. At first site this looked more like a fake beard held on by a piece of string.

And as the moonlight fell on it, this beard served as a frightening deterrent to the already stunned robber.

He shouted in alarm!

Because this extraordinary facial hair had a sparkling, cornflower blue colour!

Those who did not know that Mr Wagner, due to a wondrous slap, had fallen into the paint that was prepared at the dockside for painting a ship, could mistake him for a ghost in the moonlight.

"Well, what's it gonna be?", the victim urged the robber. "Do you want to grow old here? Give me a dollar and go to hell!... Such a moronic strovacheck."

What the expression 'strovacheck' meant in Mr Wagner's dictionary, no-one knew. His persistent, deep-set drunken state heavily hampered his ability to interpret even his own words properly.

"But understand this", shouted the robber in angry desperation, "I do not have money and I don't want to shoot you. I feel sorry for you!"

"What's that got to do with me?!... Don't you turn good for my one dollar! Just shoot!"

"I won't! And I'm warning you that if I go there…"

"Then I will kick you and the jack-knife is coming out. My large, kitchen-knife-like jack-knife. On the other hand if you stay over there, then we're back in the same place, just shoot me!... What a bang! You know what: listen here! If you have no money, pay me in kind. I will accept your revolver. I may be able to get some rum for it at the Three Red Corkscrews dining room! Well, do you accept?"

… Should I continue? Following a short, desperate argument Mr Wagner got the revolver. One cannot risk either the electric chair or a knife in his back for fifty cents. The robber was at the start of his career, merely nineteen years old; this could also count towards his impotence.

"Come then, little strovacheck!", the robber's generous victim consoled him. "You can also get a sip of rum… Oops! You could at least drink the value of the ammunition… Look, what a pretty trouser suspender!", he shouted as they set off, and he spotted a long piece of string hanging above his head from the metal frames:

"I'll take this from here, blimey… it's tied up…", and he turned to the young man sweetly: "do you by any chance have a knife on you?"

"What?", asked the robber, and he turned deadly pale. "But you… threatened me… you have a knife!"

"Don't be childish! I never in my life had a knife… Oops!… wait a second! But a revolver I now have, thank God, so just stay calm, dear strovacheck…"

And he pointed his own revolver at the angry robber.

Chapter Two

Incidentally, this unusual robbery sent the world-famous story of the found battleship on its notorious way. The victim and the robber carried on their way finally in peace, or rather the old man stumbled on. This was how the conversation, that started the course of fateful events, began:

"You must be a foreigner, because everyone knows me... Every single robber knows me so well that they don't even say 'Hi' from five feet away. Where do you come from?..." He wanted to yawn but only managed to hiccup. "You could tell me about the big wide world. My parole d'honneur, I am interested in these things!"

"I arrived from Alexandria on the Nil Marsall... But even there everyone talks about the same thing as they talk about in Oakland", said the young robber. "They're all curious, what happened to the famous André de Rémieux?"

"I could have told them that! We were locked up together in Surabaya... He was a funny chap! He was stabbed in the back last year in a pub brawl in the Buffalo Head grand café in Madrid."

"Hmm... I should hardly think so. It's about a missing ocean liner called André de Rémieux. She was carrying a group of tourists, all upper class gentlemen..."

"And some swine nicked it?", interrupted Mr Wagner with a wave. "You need to be careful at sea... I know it very well..."

This reminded him about some marching song from an opera and he started singing at the top of his voice. He lived in the topsy-turvy world of operas and gambling, in the strange rapture of the optimistic drunk. The young robber only just then realised that his strangely bearded patron was deliriously drunk. He kept talking mechanically to cover this, but in between the narrow alleyways he staggered from one side to the other, but did not let go of the revolver in his right pocket for a second, so the young marauder did not dare attack this grey, blue-bearded old robber.

And where was that pub that the old man had mentioned? The destination of their journey was inconceivable to the young man. Soon they were stumbling amongst the mounds surrounding the docks, beyond the mud houses of Frisco's Chinese and other Asian nations, the strange old man leading the way singing loudly. Was it possible that he no longer knew where he was heading?

This individual did not know Mr Wagner if he thought that the Bluebeard (in whatever state) could not find a pub he set off to go to.

"Are you lost?", asked the young robber.

"Come now!", guffawed Mr Wagner. "You baby. I would find the Three Red Corkscrews even if I was drunk, and I swear on my life I haven't had a drink for two hours… Do you see those six lights over there? No… What about those five?"

"Over there?... I only see one little light that way!..."

"I only saw one too at your age. No big deal… That's where our pub is… every worthwhile stinker goes there."

"Tell me…", asked the young robber, and this is where this whole crazy situation started. "Do you know a certain dock celebrity, a Dirty Fred? … the captain?"

"What?!...", growled the old man. "And you dare steal from honest rascals in the docks?!"

"I heard him being mentioned, too. But I thought you may know more. This captain is being sought urgently for something."

"He's always being sought!", Mr Wagner waved is hand. "But he won't be caught! He's my friend! My old Dirty Fred, the old strovacheck, the captain." He fell over a mound after an overenthusiastic wave of his hand, and remained sitting there to take a rest. He continued panting: "The police force of the whole world is twaddle for that one…"

"I don't think that a crime is in question here. They did not mention that he broke into somewhere and stole money."

"And I don't think that that old man would break into somewhere and add to the money. It's not in his nature."

He somehow got on his feet giddily and they carried on.

"There is no crime in this case. It was announced on the radio as well that he should report to any of the British ambassadors. It was guaranteed that he could leave freely."

"The ambassador?"

"Why the ambassador?"

"Why, old Fred leaves anyway if he wants to, he does not need a guarantee."

"I'm only asking because the person who knows where the captain is and reports it would get a reward of a hundred pounds immediately."

"What…" He stopped for a second, but he could only succeed in this by swinging his body wobbling on his heel forwards with rapid circling movements of his arms. "What tales are you telling here? You are, I believe, drunk! Oops! Don't worry about my hiccups!... You're saying that one can get paid ten pounds for such childishness?! In one sum?!"

13

And he became very excited, because he had never had so much money.

"I said a hundred pounds! It was even announced in San Francisco on the radio."

"Don't say so much, dear marauder!", he begged quivering, and he hiccupped three times in his excitement, which made his hat fall off, on the other hand, when he bent down for it, he tripped over it, and also dragged down the young man when trying to pull himself back up. It took some time before he finally understood clearly what was said; then he screamed at the top of his voice.

"Hurray! The person will get twenty pounds!... Don't say that it's a hundred! You must have heard it wrong. So much money only exists in mathematical theorems. But twenty, that does exist, and even twenty-four! I've seen that much before!... Goodness! I can finally get stinking drunk! Hurray!", and he threw his hat in the air, then he tottered about surprised, annoyed, but he could not see the old thing anywhere. "Well, would you look at that! My hat stayed up! Never mind!... Here, take it… your revolver!... I don't need it anymore! There is credit, plenty like the sea! This credit will not swim for long…"

Then in the deserted night he handed over the loaded revolver to the robber he had just robbed, and patted his shoulder.

"Have you heard anything about the captain?", asked the youth, when after a short consideration he decided not to shoot Mr Wagner after all with the revolver he had just been handed back.

"Of course! I spoke to him at midday!"

"Where is he?"

"That I don't know."

"Then where did you speak to him?!"

"In my apartment."

"Then you must know where he is?"

"This late at night? Out of the question. It's kind enough of me to find the way there... And report him. Well, here's the pub! Let's get inside!"

And he kicked in the door of the hut. The offensive and sweltering mix of sound, smell of thick smoke, noise and harmonica music rolled towards them. But before they could step inside, Mr Wagner suddenly staggered backwards from the doorway, banged the door shut, then grabbed the boy's arm, frightened:

"Come on! Let's run!"

And he belly flopped.

The boy did not understand what was going on. If he had, he would probably have run away fast, as the offender in this sensitive case.

Because Smiley Jimmy stood in the doorway when Mr Wagner opened it! Retreat therefore was a late instruction, because the door swung open again and Smiley Jimmy jumped...

The robber, even if he did not know what was up, reached for his revolver instinctively. To accompany his move he also received a slap and in his flight he only felt that the revolver was ripped from his hand. Then he fell and fainted. The slap he received, with its monsoon-like howl, thunderous clash and sweeping destruction was one of Smiley Jimmy's trademark slaps, that made him such a feared celebrity amongst the larger criminal classes.

Chapter Three

Why was Mr Wagner so frightened of Smiley Jimmy? Because those in the know in the underworld, including that star of slaps, knew well that Dirty Fred, whenever he happened to be in Frisco, always stayed with Mr Wagner.

And what issues did the uncrowned king of slaps have with the captain?

This stark conflict was also the subject of talk in the docks. During some notable dubious adventures it had happened that when Smiley Jimmy successfully got all of his chestnuts out of the fire, the Captain appeared all of a sudden and grabbed the dubious but well-deserved fruits of Smiley Jimmy's efforts, without so much as scorching a fingernail, usually resulting in Smiley Jimmy getting into even more trouble of some sort. They also said there was some vague, chivalrous, old business between them, too. Allegedly Smiley Jimmy kept the captain imprisoned in a crate for twenty-four hours; on another occasion the captain landed Smiley Jimmy in quarantine, when he should have been making a very important performance elsewhere. This was how the situation became poisonous to the point that Smiley Jimmy, wherever he went to, enquired about the whereabouts of the captain, claiming that they had urgent stabbing business. Therefore in Oakland he went first of all looking for Mr Wagner, so he could find his opponent through the Bluebeard.

Smiley Jimmy had already heard a couple of days before from a smuggler friend that Dirty Fred was in Frisco. Therefore he also had to know that whoever led the British authorities to his whereabouts, would receive a hundred pounds.

The reader could rightly question why Smiley Jimmy did not go straightaway to the British Embassy and claim his reward, since he knew the clue to his current residence, at Mr Wagner's apartment. He did not know the address of the Bluebeard's permanent residence though, but he could have been an informer without the exact address. It would not have counted as snitching as the captain was sought 'on business' this time with guarantee of a free leave. On the other hand he could not have been an informer as the embassy could not have done anything with this information. Because the location of Mr Wagner's apartment in Frisco was only known by about four people in the entire world, and needless to say, Smiley Jimmy was not one of those four.

In any case, the more privileged members of the underworld did not like to appear in official places for any reward. It was a superstition amongst the experienced that it led to no good sauntering about in official offices.

Smiley Jimmy had various sad experiences with the port and other authorities. Money was an important thing and it was inadvisable for anyone to be too fussy about its origin, but even this had its limit. This frigate lieutenant, as an infamous smuggler, had no qualms about stepping over limits, but the doorstep of an office was such a limit for him that he did not like to cross it of his own accord. This was why he did not report with this intelligence as an informer at the British Embassy, and that's why Mr Wagner shouted 'let's run' before he belly flopped. And that's also why he was not surprised when a clamp-like grab was placed on the back of his neck, hauling him to his feet so firmly that he could not make a move.

"Well would you look at that!", he stammered with a disfigured but polite expression. "My dear friend strovacheck!... Thank you for helping me onto my feet, and now dust me down." Since he received no answer and the clamp did not loosen, he screeched in with even more amiable smile: "Do you happen to have a cigar on you? Who knows how long ago I smoked last…"

Smiley Jimmy was wearing his especially picturesque, well-known frigate lieutenant uniform. (The rank and the uniform were his own creations.)

The uniform looked like this: first of all two splendid and shiny leather gaiters, on his head the States' volunteer rescue force's white peaked cap and gold-buttoned flannel jacket. (Those who did not know that this outfit was a frigate lieutenant uniform, could swear that they saw a smoking-jacket.) And the aristocratic, highly decorative, monocle on a handle. This was what he called that certain medical magnifying glass hanging on a bicycle chain that was otherwise used to examine an iris. Smiley Jimmy lifted this instrument from time to time to one of his eyes when he felt that he needed to present himself.

"You dirty pickpocket!", he shouted at his captive instead of a greeting. "Don't try to fool me because I'll slap you to shreds."

"Always with these shreds", fretted Mr Wagner. "Why do you ask for the fifth time where Dirty Fred is? Am I the keeper of that strovacheck?!"

"So you know what it's about?! Because I haven't even asked you yet! Don't worry; I'm not going to kill that swine! I'm just going to make him pay for that quarantine, with all he has!"

"All right! Just wait here, I'll send him over!", and he would have set off already if an iron fist did not drag him back. "Hey! You're always yanking!"

"Now listen here! I will complete the settlement with you if you don't take me to his hiding place! I know it's around the railway bridge of Frisco."

"Thank you, strovacheck! I will find my way from there!... I've been thinking hard for an hour... Stop with the yanking!"

His voice ended in gurgling as Smiley Jimmy shook him mercilessly. In the meantime the young robber came to, but did not move, because he thought that Smiley Jimmy had an iron bar with him, that he had used to hit his face. (The young man travelled to Indo-China the following day, started a new life and thereon stayed on the straight and narrow. It was too much for one mortal, to meet Mr Wagner and Smiley Jimmy on the same night.)

The frigate lieutenant was thinking with gritted teeth about what to do with Mr Wagner. He in the meantime fell asleep, supporting his weight against the grabbing fist. When he was shaken again, he snorted loudly and jerked awake:

"Good God! What time is it?!", he shouted, as if he had anything to do in his life, as if he was ever late for anywhere.

"Listen here! I will get you to a hundred pounds if you lead me to the captain."

"I'm begging you, believe me... There is no such amount of money, my son, as you're saying... That's only ten pounds! In any case the good old man Dirty Fred is no longer with me! Believe me, you strovacheck! Do I ever lie?"

"Only!"

"I'm sure it's as you say... But why would I lie now when you're holding my neck so kindly... A friend? With whom I even spent time in prison! Two fellow inmates!"

Smiley Jimmy was thinking. It was foolish to scare the sly old rascal. He would not get anything out of him. Instead he would follow him secretly, from afar. He let go of his neck and tossed him away.

"If he's not here now, I'll get him next time! And then there'll be no pardon!"

Mr Wagner bowed slightly, gallantly, straightened his flower and disappeared into the darkness, swaying. Suddenly he shouted happily because he had stepped on his hat.

"Well, this one fell back down with a long delay!", he sang to himself and put his old belonging back on. Then humming, after every ten steps sliding three or four meters on average, over mounds, through alleys, he went swaying on his way home, and it seemed that he had no idea that Smiley Jimmy was following him like a shadow.

This was how he reached the other side of the docks, beyond the dry docks, the road leading from Oakland to San Francisco. Here through empty plots he stumbled to a rampart. Along the railway tracks, he carefully turned off into the darkness, onto safer meadows.

Now!

The stumbling figure later scrambled back towards the rampart through the meadows, at a turning. He was walking around the railway sidings. Only a rail well and a few sheds were visible, and several empty carriages stood around.

What the devil!

The old man swarmed up the rampart. He lifted the latch on the door of a carriage standing farther away on an unused track, he slid the door aside and sneaked inside...

Smiley Jimmy was running! When he reached the carriage following Mr Wagner's tracks, he approached carefully... It paid to be careful... He took out his torch and looked around...

So he lived together with the captain in this rusty, castoff wagon. Let's go then! He would make him pay... He quickly pulled the door aside and jumped inside... His torchlight spun around quickly because Dirty Fred's hands were fast...

What's this?!

The inside of the wagon was empty!

He jumped to the sliding door on the opposite side... The devil! This Wagner had simply jumped out on the other side and locked it from the outside!

Up! He turned around with lightning speed...

Too late! A loud grinding noise came from behind him, from the way he had come...

And that wagon door slammed shut! He heard it clearly when the latch fell in place.

He was a prisoner!

"Hallo, my friend strovacheck!... Every wagon has two doors", screeched Mr Wagner from the outside. "You'll need to hammer on the door a lot when you get bored because this carriage has been delayed recently: it hasn't left for five years..."

And a receding, enthusiastic song was heard about a chorus-girl called Aida, who first fooled the green jack and then played the red queen...

Chapter Four

Smiley Jimmy was in big trouble.

He would starve here if he did not bang on the door. On the other hand his current situation in Frisco was such that it was not advisable for him to bring attention to himself by making a lot of noise. Unfortunately, last time here he had departed on a two-master schooner with Moonlight Charley and they forgot to bring it back to its owner, who must have got the police looking for it by now.

What use was the screwdriver in his inside pocket, the outstanding quality, small, splendid steel drill in his upper pocket, the pliers and the file in his back pocket? He could not break out by cold-chiselling, he knew it well. He was an old acquaintance of wagons.

He could perhaps file away the latch through the gap along the door, but this would make a louder noise than banging on it. He sat around for about an hour, fuming, deep in thought, out of ideas. He saw around the latch that dawn was approaching.

The shuffling sound of evenly spaced steps came around the wagon.

He listened. Perhaps some lonely person was walking around here, and maybe inexperienced enough to open the door?

He would try it. After all he did not intend to starve to death in here. He knocked…

"Come in!", said the person outside.

To hell with his joking mood!

"Open up!", shouted Smiley Jimmy, "I missed the Frisco train, I slept here and someone locked the door on me, I'm a dock labourer!"

At this the person opened the door without further ado.

Smiley Jimmy, also without further ado, stepped back, and slammed onto an empty crate with his mouth wide open. Heavens!

A person with a long, pointy goat beard stood at the door, and with his unrealistically long, hawk-like claws he was twisting this impressive beard to be even pointier. There was no doubt!

The captain stood there! Dirty Fred was his rescuer!

And Smiley Jimmy saw his fate sealed. If this man had saved him, then he was a lost man! No doubt...

"I heard, my son, that you were looking for me... You must have some business with me ", he said kindly.

Gosh!... How easy it was to be searching for him to put his knife in him. And now what's all this about that he found himself at last sitting here all uncertain opposite this weather-beaten, thousand-wrinkled old man. What sort of enchanting power or magical authority those small, slyly shining eyes held, that this first-class knifer, this Hercules-strong, maniacal fighter should be so hesitant? He smiled a little, started stammering, and finally primly flipped something off his jacket with his two fingers to cover his embarrassment. But he eventually pulled himself together, since he had already sworn on heaven and earth that he should never again see Pepita Ophelia, his (supposedly) faithful betrothed, if he did not finish the captain.

"The thing here is", he said, leading himself on with his aggressive tone, "that I have business to finish with you!"

23

"Is that so?!... What's the thing, then?", he asked, and suddenly stepped towards him.

A small scratch, as if a thorn brushed his skin through his shirt, tickled the frigate lieutenant's stomach area.

"Be careful, Jimmy!...", warned the captain with a tender whisper. "It's dark in here, and you may accidentally walk into my knife."

… How he took out his knife, when he opened it and how he pressed it against his stomach with such expertise that it touched but did not penetrate? This was an old and mysterious magic trick of his. One thing was certain: one could be a hundred Smiley Jimmies, but if Dirty Fred's knife tip was touching his stomach, it was better that he had the last sacrament administered, before he moved so much as his little finger.

"What are you waving a knife about for?... Has anyone hurt you?", Smiley Jimmy asked a lot more rudely, but without moving an inch.

"Just because I heard that you've been looking for me for something, and I'm interested in the nature of the case."

"What?... And what if I did? The owner of the Happy Blower-out from Hawaii sent you a message that you left your tobacco pouch there last year…"

"I know about that. It's so nice of you to look for me for about a year for that, sometimes in the Catacomb Casino in Singapore, as they said, and sometimes in the Cheeseheaded Roller in Rotterdam, because I've been informed of that too… Is it all worth it for a tobacco pouch?"

Smiley Jimmy almost exploded in his rage, but what could he do when he was standing there speared onto the old man's knife tip, and he knew that the knife was laid in the captain's hand steadily, loose, slightly at an angle on his palm, and the blade ready to stab snuggled up against his outstretched thumb. And how simply, easily, with a lightning speed it could slide into someone, and that Dirty Fred would wipe it on a tree trunk afterwards, put it in his pocket, and with indifferent, swaying steps he would walk away from the scene.

So the frigate lieutenant swelled up in anger, but at the same time he stood there motionless, almost piously, as if he had been really only looking for this respectable, but mighty old bearded individual all over the world just because of his tobacco pouch.

"And you also said that you had an account to settle with me, supposedly", enquired the captain gently. "I don't know if it's true? Well, I don't mind, you can give it to me now."

"I haven't got it with me… I had it when I was looking for you and…"

The old man left him and sat down on a log a bit further away, pocketing his knife.

"Well, listen here, Smiley Jimmy!", he said deep in thought, but determinedly, after a short pause. "It is all very nice what you've been telling me here; but note that if someone is persistently looking for me, it can happen that he should find me accidently." He was talking calmly, because Smiley Jimmy knew well that with the same unnoticeable move that he put the knife away, he could pull it out again. "You know well that I have always had a soft spot for you… Just walk like that, my son, up and down, put your hands in your pocket if you like, you had a revolver and a knife which I stole from you earlier. Don't grind your teeth like that because they will all fall out by the time you reach my age, and even at this age it doesn't hurt to have them."

"One day I will…"

"Don't you threaten me, because I got scared before when you were angry, and I had a restless sleep."

He was pondering about something, and picking a few browned teeth sticking out of his lower jaw with the long fingernail of his thumb, than he set about leisurely stuffing his pipe and lit it.

'He's cooking something up again!', thought Smiley Jimmy. 'He did not come here to rescue me, because he was worried about me. Even his own brother could drop dead for all he cares, the dog that he is. And now he's sitting here smoking away, while his brain is working out how to stir things up, and no man on earth could figure it out apart from him.'

'Because he is always stirring things!', thought the frigate lieutenant. But he should give up his knife altogether if he doesn't put it in this Satan someday.

"Do you want anything else from me?", he asked angrily.

"I would like to settle our account in a way that you would leave me alone from now on."

"Are you making fun?! You can do it now, but remember this, even the slyest fox gets caught one day."

"Well, I would very much like to avoid that", nodded the captain seriously. "I would like to make a business deal with you in a way that both you and I have fifty pounds each."

"What's this again, then?"

"I will tell you. The British Embassy is looking for me for some business. This search does not have consequences. Perhaps they have questions about the sunken steamer Winifred, because I happened to sail that way with a three-master and I saved many of the passengers."

"I remember that. It was a great deed. Only afterwards everyone was surprised that the passengers rescued from the storm lost their rings and pocket watches as well."

"Yes!", nodded the captain with a serious look of remembrance. "It was a great storm… But the matter at hand is that I would probably receive a reward if I reported at the embassy, and the informer, who found me, would get a hundred pounds. Now I would like to receive fifty out of this hundred on top of my own reward. Therefore you will take me to the embassy, you would receive fifty pounds, and I would also strike a bargain because I no longer need to worry about you killing me one day. Because I hope that this way peace can be settled between us."

'Is he scheming or not?' What he said sounded plausible enough, therefore it was certain that he was lying. But what did he gain by stirring up trouble with him? Was it possible that the old man really wanted peace and fifty pounds? He could not get into trouble from agreeing to it. He wouldn't be questioned there about his name, and even if he was, he had excellent papers in the name of Jeff Olsen, a Swedish sailor, in his inside pocket. He would go there with the old man as Jeff Olsen and he would keep his eyes open.

"I think", he said carefully, after a short while thinking, "that there is some swinishness against me behind all this again."

"If you are so mistrustful, I will do it with someone else. I see that you're scared."

Smiley Jimmy had many virtues, but his vanity sometimes easily supressed his other qualities. Hearing the accusation of being a coward made him turn red yet again.

"Have you ever heard that I was afraid of anyone?! You are talking to Smiley Jimmy here you know!"

"I also based everything on this myself", said the old man honestly, and this was how it was too. He often counted on Smiley Jimmy's vanity and naivety in his plans. "So if you want, you may now come with me to my hiding place. Few people on this earth know where it is, I'll let you be one of them. And in the morning we will visit the embassy. You will receive your fifty pounds and peace will be settled between us. Here's my hand!"

He extended his mummy-like, dirty brown hawk's-claw of a hand for a handshake.

Smiley Jimmy thought to himself: 'Is he stirring it, or not stirring it?', and he hesitantly accepted the extended hand. This hooligan, feared around the docks, with his extraordinary wide chest, his wonderful slickness and legendary strength, took the cool, wrinkled, relatively small hand so nervously and hesitantly, as a school kid would shake the hand of a strict teacher.

"Do you have any papers?", asked the captain.

"A good document, in the name of Jeff Olsen."

"It's all right then, although I don't think we'll be needing it."

The old man set off ahead of him, smoking his pipe, with swaying steps, his coat over his arm, his thumb pushed on the peak of his hat so the ancient piece of clothing slid back over the back of his head.

They reached the outskirts of Frisco not far from the bridge, and Smiley Jimmy thought it was a bad omen to see the grey stone building of the gendarmes' barracks. Well, he would not hide around here. They melted further into the semidarkness around the rampart along the railway, because it was getting lighter by now. It was quite cold around here at this time of the year, especially at dawn. The arctic wind chased away the dock wayfarers towards the end of the summer.

A freezing, salty breeze slapped them. 'This old tanned robber probably doesn't even feel it', thought Smiley Jimmy. Around a bend along the highway, Dirty Fred lifted the grille of a drain and started climbing down the metal steps.

"Come on!", he shouted back up.

Smiley Jimmy followed him, putting the grille back neatly in its place above his head. Were they living in the sewers? He could believe that of that Wagner, but the captain (to give him his due), knew what he owed to his reputation and his dirty, but peaked cap. He would not allow rumours to be spread about him that he lived in the sewers. They walked along the concrete path by the fast flowing sewer water for a long time. They forever had to kick away the rats swarming around their feet. A cat-sized beast jumped across Smiley Jimmy's face and landed with a splash in the water.

Soon they reached a cross junction and the captain headed upwards. They went through another grille and they reached Dirty Fred's hiding place.

Crikey!

It was a spacious cellar. All around them various bundles of rags lay, providing a comfortable bed for the hideaways.

"What sort of a cellar is this?", asked Smiley Jimmy and...

The sound got stuck in his throat. On the other side of the cellar, high up, there were a few windows, and grey morning light seeped through them. Outside the window suddenly two suspiciously firm steps appeared... A few steps and a thud... turned...a slap... and headed away with even, firm steps again...

This was a guard post! The captain had led him into a trap!

This was his first thought and he jumped immediately back towards the sewer grille.

He cowered there panting... No! Dirty Fred could not have led him into a trap. The old devil had just as much to account for with the authorities as he did. Look!... He sat down, pulled a piece of cheese out of his pocket in front of him and started eating with a good appetite...

"Uncle Freddy...", he stuttered. "Where are we here?"

"This, my son, is the cellar of the gendarmes' barracks. A storage cellar, nobody comes here, they just throw in the unusable, dissipated things through the window, and once a year the state rag collector comes with a van to take them. It's a quiet place. I've never heard of a raid taking place in here."

... And he laid down onto a bunch of stale rags and immediately fell into a deep sleep.

Chapter Five

They left the cellar early in the morning to head to Frisco.

"Where are you engaged these days?", asked the captain on the way, and despite the ice cold, real Frisco August wind he did not put his coat on. His black cotton sweater, with its frayed neck, had been hardened to an armour-like thickness during its weather-beaten life, and it seemed that it adequately protected its owner in the battle against the weather. Not to mention his plank-like, chest-high, notoriously enormous trousers, with their ends tucked neatly into his shoes…

"Well, I served with Captain Breeches", replied Smiley Jimmy. "We smuggled migrants on the schooner Setoff into Java."

"That's been a year", said the old man lighting his pipe.

"Well then", he replied annoyed, "I've also been indisposed! When the schooner Setoff was finished, I got a bullet in my hip, and I swam with it from one island of Sunda to another. Human constitution is such that if one takes exercise with a bullet wound, one will get sick. Now do you know everything?!"

"Well, perhaps. It's been over a year since you said good bye to Pepita Ophelia one night and arrived in Frisco on Dork Harry's cargo ship."

This man has made a pact with the devil! Otherwise how could he know everything?

"So what? I came over to Frisco? And?! Have you changed career to become a police commissioner so now you're interrogating me?! Do you publish your every step in the newspapers?! Ridiculous… One must make a living, so one travels…"

Dirty Fred said nothing, shrugged his shoulders, nudged his cap, wriggled his trousers up to his armpits by the pockets, and stared into empty air somewhere, looking bored. Smiley Jimmy looked sideways at him nervously from time to time. Now he really could not know anything more. He could only be asking around like this stabbing in the dark, because he was walking with his toes turned in, grumpily, like always. They were walking in the Golden Gate Park, in a real city environment, when all of a sudden Dirty Fred asked with a unexpectedly soft expression:

"Where would my old fellows be, I wonder? Have you heard about the battleship Radzeer? Did you hiccup?"

"Yes. This is a strong cigarette. What did you ask again?"

"I remembered the good old battleship Radzeer, which I stole on a dark stormy night from around Point de Galle, from the quarantine in Ceylon." He let out a big sigh. "Those good old days!"

He was the world's best actor, but he would not be acting like this. It had to be a complete coincidence that he should mention the Radzeer.

"I have not seen that ship yet", replied the frigate lieutenant coldly.

"Hmm… well, have you got good eyes then? It was tied up in Oakland about half a year ago. Did you not notice it?"

Smiley Jimmy stopped. He filled his enormous chest with air. Few people remained in the vicinity when he did this, if they knew him.

"Now what mischief are you plotting here again?!"

"You're strange…", the captain shrugged his shoulders while stuffing his pipe. "You are socialising with people more than I do, so I simply thought that you may have bumped into the Professor, Moonlight Charley, Spikey Vanek and the others while they moored there with the old cruiser, and you were also in Oakland furthering your livelihood here. Why do you work yourself up so much about this?"

Smiley Jimmy deflated his chest. He was always wary of this heartless weasel and always thought that he was getting at something. After all, what was wrong with enquiring about his old friends? True that he spat on them last time and said that they could drop dead for all he cared, and like many times before, he left them and set off alone, but that time the issue was that as usual, he had manipulated the oil and all sorts, faked the ship's logbook and cheated them. They also said that the devil brought him into their way all the time, the rotten-larynxed Petters called the captain a parricidal old hyena, but a friend was a friend after all. Even if not all of them were a ruler like he, Smiley Jimmy, therefore they could not know the official expressions of Spanish court etiquette.

Of course he had noticed, whilst in Frisco, that the Radzeer was moored there, and it was quite stupid to say he didn't see it. Was there anything in Oakland, no matter how small, that Smiley Jimmy did not spot when he walked along the docks? Therefore he had given a stupid response. That's all.

"Well", he replied with forced indifference, "I spoke to Spikey Vanek and some of the others. But it's not important. And I'm not going to blab it out to anyone what it was, because my livelihood…"

"I know, son", he nodded understandingly. "You may have mentioned that already. I only wanted to find out where did the cruiser go from here? It's been six months since I've last heard about where the ship docked and I'm worried…"

"What?... Did you leave your silverware or your tobacco pouch there?"

"I'm worried about my friends."

"Look, captain, leave me alone! It's fine that you're always drunk, but it seems that recently this has started to show in your speech. What sort of friends do you have in this world, with your stone cold heart?"

"Jimmy, Jimmy! Who else would make you come into fifty pounds with the intention of making peace?"

This was true after all. If only he wasn't asking things like this. Because not even God Almighty knew what he was thinking when he was asking questions like this.

"If you're dying of curiosity, I can tell you what Busy Weasel told me before they left. An insurance company paid them again, to look after a valuable ship."

"Strange!", the captain muttered again after a short pause. "Well, never mind… hmm… extremely strange…"

"What's strange for you again?"

"Here is Smiley Jimmy, the world's best sailor! I know something about this, so you can believe me. And today, when a common sailor is worth gold in Frisco, he is being ignored and the Radzeer leaves without him. The devil understands this. Or is it now common knowledge that you're not the same anymore? That's possible… Someone mentioned it to me as well the other day."

"That is a foul lie!" He suddenly came to his senses. This old sea monster was prodding at his vanity again. "Well now, they did call me, and I didn't go because I am at odds with Fat Petters. Now you know?!" .

34

The captain shrugged, and spat out next to his pipe with a sideways spit:

"Why are you so stroppy? You didn't go, so you didn't go…"

And he scratched the back of his head with his no. 2 habitual move, which made his cap move forward on his head. They were walking along quietly. The British Consulate appeared in the distance. All of a sudden someone shrieked next to them:

"Here is my good old friend!... By God! I can have my twenty-two pounds!"

It was Mr Wagner! With an embassy official!

Smiley Jimmy swore. This wretched Wagner had got there before them. And now whether they wanted it or not, the money was his. The Bluebeard, the old scoundrel was leaning against the wall with his right hand, but in the heat of his drunkenness he had to grab the hat of the embassy official to steady himself, and he tore off half the rim. He had obviously already received a bottleful as advance.

"Are you the notorious individual called 'Captain'?", asked the embassy official.

"Pardon?", asked the captain surprised. "I don't understand. I am a common sailor."

"But my dear friend!", screamed Mr Wagner, splashing his hands together despairingly, then he wanted to hug one of the Dirty Freds out of the six, but he fell forward onto the pavement at full length, which barely bothered him, and this way he could continue his complaints in a more stable, comfortable position: "How could you say something like that?... I swear, it is him, put him in chains!"

"Who is this drunken animal?", asked the captain calmly, and the frigate lieutenant on one hand was amazed by this insolence, on the other he revered him as he already saw through Dirty Fred's ingenious plan.

"He reported to me saying that he lives together with you in a cellar."

"I've never seen this person. Here, this is my identification. I arrived here a week ago from Aden, on the Göterborg, I am the sailor Jeff Olsen."

What's this?!

The captain calmly took out Smiley Jimmy's almost real document from his inside pocket and handed it to the enquirer… Two minutes later they left hurriedly, and they rushed to get away from the area as Mr Wagner, clutching the torn off half rim of the embassy official's hat to his heart, was chasing after them crying, until he fell over onto the ground so favourably that he fell asleep.

Chapter Six

"If we go to the embassy, this official will say that the reward is due to this Wagner after all."

"Then we won't go in. You'll send a note to the consul in which you request that he would receive us."

"According to court custom", explained Smiley Jimmy, remembering his short rule over The Blissful Isles, "sermon procedure is that usually a request for hearing is submitted to the king's cabin office."

"You just do as I say."

In the evening Dirty Fred and Smiley Jimmy appeared in the English consul's flat in Frisco, where they were immediately led into a small salon-like room. Two gentlemen were waiting for them there. Smiley Jimmy had spent two years in the navy when he was a stripling, and it was after this that his inability to live without the smell of the sea arose. Therefore he immediately recognised one of those present as rear admiral Anderson. The other one was Haynes, the consul. The consul did not ask which one of them was Dirty Fred. Only a blind man would not realise that.

"Finally, you've been found, dear Captain!", he said with honest happiness.

The rear admiral had once served along with Fred as cadets on His Highness the Prince of Buckingham's warship, a fact that perhaps only the two of them knew in the world. It was said that the captain was roaming the sea because of some hazy, never fully uncovered family tragedy, shedding his captain's uniform and his more distinguished life. Since then occasionally, in cases that could not be pursued officially, where even the Secret Service was perplexed, Dirty Fred was hunted up from some remote corner of the world, to make use of his unique experiences and extraordinary crookedness.

This usually did not go smoothly.

The misanthropic, lonely sea wolf would not toe the line if it was not Anderson calling him. Did the old man have a heart after all? Perhaps...

It was strange that this extremely tight, greedy man simply disappeared after these assignments, and he could not be found anywhere to hand over his reward.

"Welcome, Fred!", the admiral greeted him and put his hand on his shoulder. The old man murmured something and stuffed his hat in his pocket. Smiley Jimmy, who had turned quite formal after his mingling in royal circles (according to him), lifted his handled monocle to his left eye and bowed.

"This here", the captain introduced him, "is Smiley Jimmy, the world's best sailor."

The frigate lieutenant blushed at this praise. It seemed that there was some humanity in that dog that he sympathized with him. The fifty pounds was now certain.

"In all honesty, it is not information that we want from you", said council Haynes to the captain, "we would like to make use of your services."

"This young man notified me that you were looking for me, so the reward is due to him", said the captain, "I would like to hand over the hundred pounds to him personally for his eagerness."

"Here, I have already prepared it", smiled Haynes, and he counted the sum out in dollars. Smiley Jimmy was slightly surprised when the old man nodded towards him with an encouraging smile, but put the money in his own pocket.

"This is yours, Jimmy, because you did well", and he sat down, because the rear admiral offered them a seat with a wave of his hand. "I'm curious why you were looking for me?"

"Have you heard of the ship called André de Rémieux?"

"A double-funnelled, fifteen tonne steamer, christened in Cherbourg seventeen years ago. Since then she has only required repairs once, following the Mael-torrent in Penang. She was in dry dock in Batavia. Recently she headed to Incognita Archipelago with some tourists and disappeared. The last radio signal was sent from the altitude of Point Blount.

"You know everything, Fred", said the rear admiral satisfied, "do you perhaps have any idea what happened to the steamer?"

Smiley Jimmy looked at the old man nervously, but he just shrugged his shoulders wonderingly:

"Is there anyone in this world who would know what could happen to a missing ship beyond Point Blount? In any case, what does an intelligent man want around there with a steamer? Beyond the Marquesas there are only coral and atoll reefs and atoll and coral reefs again down to the South Pole."

"We know, we know!", nodded Anderson. "Unfortunately a few rich and aristocratic people sailed there for a bet. They wanted to be Robinson Crusoes. They decided that they would spend a few years on the Incognita Archipelago. Some scatty painter arrived from there and he said that the island was like a real paradise."

"Have you intercepted any emergency signals?"

"No. The last transmission came from the latitude of Point Blount that everything was in order. The foolish Robinson Crusoes were approaching their destination in bright weather.

No other news came from them. It was only later that it transpired that their insurance company had hired the Radzeer to follow them. The strange thing is that the Radzeer also sent her last transmission from a few degrees beyond Cape Blount, and then her radio went silent. Both ships disappeared. It is your task, Fred... to bring news from them."

"I'm sorry, sir", said the captain coldly and stood up. "I have already agreed with a whaler. We're leaving next week to the Portola Islands. It is said that cetaceans are teeming around there."

"Why do you not accept the assignment to search for the Radzeer and the Robinsons?"

"Because it is not impossible that I will find them and I would rather avoid that", he said grumpily. Smiley Jimmy felt ashamed that this greedy old Satan spoke like this to the gentlemen. The admiral commented moodily:

"I thought that it was your old friends who were sailing that ship."

"That's incorrect, sir! I only had trouble with them, they always blamed me for everything. Disagreeable fellows. Not a drop of seawater is worth being disturbed for them..."

And he wriggled his trousers so that he sunk into them up to his armpits again.

"Well, I'm sorry...", said the consul. "Do you at least have an opinion on the case?"

"What sort of opinion could there be? Someone should sail nine and a half degrees east at Cape Blount and look around from the crow's nest. If neither steamer is visible, than you won't know in a thousand years what happened to your ships. The Green Bloke has not said so far how deep down he takes the south-pacific ocean liners if any of them annoy him."

'What a dirty dog he is', thought Smiley Jimmy, 'but he talks in a way as if his every word is scripture!'

The admiral was looking at Dirty Fred's cold, disinterested face searchingly. Did the two small eyes flash his way? Or did it just look like that in the light coming from the chandelier?

"Well... I'm not forcing the issue, Fred..."

"If you listen to me, sir, then you should appoint this sailor, who brought me here, instead of me. I know whom I'm recommending. This is such a man that he could sail to the pole with a rowboat and a single sail and back."

Smiley Jimmy turned bright red. He was not such a big dog after all as he thought!

The admiral would have liked to look behind Fred's face with his stare. But he looked back at him calmly and sternly. Anderson turned to the consul:

"Even if we have to go without the captain's service, we should accept his recommendations." And he stepped to Smiley Jimmy.

"Come and see me tomorrow in the Waldorf Astoria. Everything you need will be ready for you for the expedition. The insurance company offered a reward of fifty thousand dollars for the one bringing sure information about the missing ships. On top of that you can also expect a separate reward, from high up..."

Smiley Jimmy felt his over-fanned vanity overwhelmed. Therefore he put his handled monocle to his eye again and bowed deeply. Meanwhile from his time as king he remembered a recorded quotation by a well-known colleague of his named Napoleon, and said:

"Please... with iron and bread I would even reach China."

"Don't brag, Jimmy", the captain snubbed him, "because you have already reached China more than once, without a single piece of bread or iron."

The hearing finished with this, the admiral shook hands with Fred:

"If you change your mind, Fred…"

The captain said disdainfully:

"I'm only going after whales. Those animals are better than some humans. And more importantly, far more useful. I shall have nothing to do with those chaps who accused me and were so ungrateful to me…"

When they got to the street, Smiley Jimmy said with honest gratefulness:

"Thank you, uncle Freddy… and now give me the fifty pounds."

"You beggar! Since when do you deserve fifty pounds?... Or do you want to get rich on my account? Is it not enough that I earned you fifty thousand dollars? That's easy to get."

"You promised", he said angrily, "that half of the money…"

"All right. When you return and you give me half of the fifty thousand dollars, you will get the fifty pounds from me. I've had enough of you, now go to hell while I'm in a good humour."

That said, he thrust his hands in his pockets, turned around and he did not even look back at the frigate lieutenant, as he waddled off towards the docks…

Chapter Seven

Smiley Jimmy walked through the docks. He looked at the mass of ships passingly. Even in the biggest docks there were no more than three ships that were worth doing business with.

The rest were only good enough for the storage closet.

These beautiful, two and three funnel steamers, bearing the symbols of big companies, were not worth the attention. Firstly, a ship was not worth half if one did not know her 'personally' from the engine to the ropes. Secondly, these constructions were just fops. Painted beautifully, with shiny railings and splendidly large light bulbs, but if a little larger than usual storm came at sea, the whole shebang would sink so that not even a splinter was left on the surface of the sea an hour later.

He went past some schooners or cutters bearing yellow, red and black or colourful sails, with more passion.

How do you like that!

For example there was the Yankee-Doodle. And next to her the Seehund. With these it was easy to overcome the trials of the sea, even where it was the most dangerous. The youngest of these worn, enormous sailing boats was at least fifty years old; on their frames every sea of the world was represented by some moss or lighter patches here and there: the signs of repairs following heavy storms. These were usually done impromptu, because there was no hurricane or cyclone that made a ship like this go into dry dock because of the damage. It was also true that these ships were built from jarrah wood from top to bottom. Not even a hundred years is enough for the sea to wear out a big structure like that.

Look! There was the La Bahia! He would hire it on the spot. Of course, the captain Spanish Jose would only laugh if some fool tried to borrow his ship. He was a Spaniard with a shaggy black beard and torn vest. He was leaning onto the railings, wearing trousers that were rolled up to his knees, spitting at the fish.

Over there was the Drummer Dogg, also unobtainable. The captain, old Ruff, was not bothered about anything but collecting copra. He went wandering around the archipelago like some peddler, to load his ship with a cargo of dried coconuts, and pining for the old times when there was fierce shooting and axe fights too.

Around the free docks, amongst the various sized ships, his gaze finally rested on a dinky, tar coloured, tattered shell of a steamer. She was anchored far back close to the stone wall, where the ships for hire were anchored.

But this was the Hountler!

With this he could sail around the worthwhile sailing routes and the waters ten times. One who had not signed on this ship before, would not even think that. He hurried to the Hountler; hopefully there would be someone on board to give him some information?

There was.

More people than it would have been comfortable. Two sailors: the bearded Snout Eugene; the one nicknamed Generous Rothschilds and a few others. They were hammering, tying knots; it was indubitable that the ship was already hired. They were just loading the compressed-air whaling guns. It was certain that the old man was sailing on the Hountler for whaling.

Two sailors were carrying a crate decorated with a lot of skulls and crossbones to the cargo hall. These crates stored those pointy grenades that they secured onto the tip of the harpoons, because nowadays they shot whales with these.

The Hountler had been fished out from under his nose by the Captain. And Smiley Jimmy knew well that another decent ship that he could sail with beyond Cape Blount was not lain up in Frisco... The frigate lieutenant sighed. Even the best men were hired by this Satan before him.

"Hey, Chang!", he shouted up to the bearded sailor.

"What is it?"

"What other decent ship can be found around here?"

"The captain sent you a message", shouted back the sailor, "because he knew you would be coming here to goggle. He said: Go back to the Three-Mast Soda inn. The Blind Dad is coming in from quarantine tonight because her closure is finished. Impertinent Manfred lends it out!"

Smiley Jimmy went running. So this captain was not so black-hearted after all. Impertinent Manfred's ship was just as good as the Hountler. The Blind Dad did not look bigger than a propeller, and the superficial observer would believe that she belonged in an antique shop rather than at sea, but if someone had ever been chased by two warships on this old sock he would know what to think of her. In one word the Blind Dad ten-thousand tonne steamer, the property of Impertinent Manfred, was mentioned with respect in every dock.

The bearded, fat, one-eyed captain was no longer at the Three-Mast Soda inn. Where was he? The waiter said that a boy came for him, and he was called away somewhere.

Would you believe that!

Someone may yet get ahead of him. He went outside and looked around to see where to start looking for Manfred.

There!

He was standing about twenty feet away in front of a lamppost and looking at something on the ground. As he got closer that something turned out to be Mr Wagner. The Bluebeard, due to his condition, could not go further than the post, that's why he had sent for the captain. Smiley Jimmy ran and said panting:

"Hallo, Manfred! How much for the Blind Dad? I need her for a zexpedition."

"…My dear friend strovacheck! I'm sorry that you're late!... What a pleasure!..." Mr Wagner said with outpouring enthusiasm, and he managed to stagger upright by the pole with small climbing movements of his hands. "What do you think, I've hired the ship from this one?... The deaf…, the lame, yes, the lame father named ship…"

"You're late, Jimmy!", nodded Manfred as well. "This moron really hired the ship. She's his for two months."

The captain left at this, and Smiley Jimmy, steaming with anger, looked at Mr Wagner, who managed to stand up from his sitting position by the exercise of climbing.

"What the devil do you need the Blind Dad for?"

"You're asking me this, you rascal?...", he kissed Smiley Jimmy, and a few steps away he started the exercise of standing up again. He pulled his hat further back on his head, so much so that the rim now went down to his neck, and hung there separately, like some oval frame of a painting of a sky blue beard. "I'm going to find my dear friends! I'm sailing after the Radzeer to Point Blount with the Blind Mom!"

And he started off, but after the first step he grabbed onto the side of a mule cart, which pulled him along so that he thumped to the ground like an old wool sack, but he was sniggering.

"Look at the foolish mule, what a hurry he's in… You, strovacheck! To show how much I think of you as a friend, I will take you in as a partner!... Well?! You can also come with that whatsit… ship… some sick relative…"

Smiley Jimmy's blood boiled with anger. This was the work of that fiend Dirty Fred! He knew that there was no decent ship in Frisco apart from the Blind Dad, so he had hired it just to skin him, because it was foreseeable that it would be needed for the expedition. Mr Wagner was only a tool in the plan.

"What right do you have to do that?! Who charged you with the search?!"

"My dear friend…", and the tottered, with open arms, weeping, "my foolish big heart and philanthropy dictates it!... And nobody can forbid me this!... My sweet friends disappeared with the Blind Dad and now they're waiting for Mr Wagner to come for them… This is why I hired the deaf parent…"

"Just say simply, you scoundrel, that the captain wants to skin me, because he knows I need the ship and there isn't another one. How much do you want to hand her over?"

"Don't even say such horrible things! There's no such money in the world… But the captain did allow that if you pay the entire sum, you can come along and you'll receive half of the fifty – hundred dollars… I beg you, don't say a thousand!", he put his hands together crying. "You're all fools, including the captain… That consul drank something beforehand and his tongue slipped… Fifty thousand dollars does not exist, not even forty thousand…"

Should I get into details? Despite the words of the festively drunk Mr Wagner, Smiley Jimmy understood what was going on. This captain was even more of a dog than he imagined, because he wanted to get his hands on half of the reward too.

(The only person whose money Mr Wagner did not dare to spend.) And he even made him pay the hire charge. Because he knew that rear admiral Anderson would supply everything generously. If only that old pirate would come along with his plentiful brain. But that Satan was going whale hunting on the Hountler.

How come some storm did not destroy this slippery, hairy-hearted scoundrel?

They went back together to the Three-Mast Soda where Smiley Jimmy first of all ordered a bucket of water and dipped Mr Wagner's head in it several times.

Then they came to an agreement.

What could he have done? Even if there was another good ship in the harbour, he could not tolerate another expedition to search after the missing ones. It was no small game being played here. As far as Smiley Jimmy knew. He had to be very careful! When Smiley Jimmy wanted to leave, Mr Wagner sang after him:

"Wait, my dove strovacheck... You are a big rascal that everyone respects... So I tell you to hurry over to the Three Red Corkscrews."

"Why the hell should I go to the Corkscrews?"

Mr Wagner grabbed a tablecloth and pulled off a few bottles and glasses. Smiley Jimmy unwrapped him from the tablecloth with some difficulty, stood him up again and repeated the question:

"Why should I go to the Corkscrews?"

"Oh, my dear strovacheck!... I clearly forgot to tell you that in terms of the person of the captain of the ship there is a mess-up and everything..."

Smiley Jimmy felt as if he was hit on the head. It was more important than anything to him to be the captain.

"What are you babbling here?!"

"Thank you for shaking me, because I'm covered with dust... The thing is here that the owner of the ship named Blind Parent would only lend her with one condition... Hallo, strovacheck, bring me rum!"

"Speak clearly or I will smash your head in!"

"Am I not speaking clearly?!... I'm speaking... so clearly... that you can turn off the lights when I speak! The owner of the ship... would only lend that big pen if we took over the cap... I'm suffocating like this..."

"The owner of the ship is One-eyed Manfred! I spoke to him!"

"But he already lent the ship to another owner and took me on as partner because he likes me a lot." And he burst into tears. "And he knows... that I want to go after my friends! My dear friends disappeared on the Radzeer... Spiky Vanek, Petters and Smiley Jimmy... But that one's not a loss..."

And he drank someone's rum sobbing, which resulted in an argument. Smiley Jimmy slowly started to understand everything. The ship already had a hirer, and One-eyed Manfred had convinced him to take this half-wit Mr Wagner on as partner.

And this person was the current captain of the ship.

Therefore his position as captain was in jeopardy. Which he had made his own since his last voyage, when he had been first mate. He even had a business card:

| Don Smiley St James |
| Ship's captain |

What did being a quartermaster mean to an ambitious man? Especially when he had already been a captain once before! In any case he had to go to the Corkscrews to sort this issue out. Whoever that captain was, he would deal with him if he stood in his way. When he got to the inn, he had a big surprise:

"I'm looking for the captain of the Blind Dad", he said to the innkeeper.

"The Captain waited for you for a while here and will come back later. Half past seven. I recommend that you behave carefully because that one does not stand for nonsense."

"Do you think there is any lad I would back away from?"

"That one is not a lad at all but a girl, and she's called Pirate Pepi."

Smiley Jimmy nearly fainted.

So the captain of the Blind Dad was a woman!

Chapter Eight

Majestic

Ruler King Samtantonio Highness

Blessingisland

Half floor, Royal Castle, to the left

Honourable Sir Kyng!

Took my fountan pen one day in running month to break it in from fellowship politeness I write a letter, as in: Your Higness, respectable heir to the throne, her honourable queen and pleasant empress mother. Because Your Hignes said on highest late card that you always take my lines with pleasure. I am much obliged at tat because Your Hignes is a king afterall which is a very high occupation.

And I have tings to say too.

Becase, the worlds eye is listening about me in the radio again. Your Hignes confessed before that you know what gentlemen duty is and not snitch on anything I said, therefore I write about this swindle as well. It was like that becase of a hip injury I had to spend a little time swimming between the islands of Sunda group. (A very dangerous shipping root, full of reefs and on top the customs police shoot at everyone.)

When my recovery was completed I went to Frisco. Here I met friend Vanek called Spiky. And our old close friend Busy Weasel was with him. They were happy to see me because they won't take just anyone on the Radzeer. Not only a good sailor is needed there but had to be a trusted accomplice. So I also signed on along them. They had a contracted trip to Ingobnito Archipel.

I am informing you, but god forbid that you let know your superintendent or draftsman friends. Becase since then the Radzeer is lost altogether, or as they say: topsy-turvy disappeared! And the other ship too, that André Demio named. And nobody knows how just us. Your Highness is the only living ear-witness of this from my letter. Because here there is such a miracle and with that detto such swindle joined together, for some coincidence that never happened before since the earth stands. And this is spinning in space for a long time.

It started with the thing that the passengers of Deremio ship were not allowed to be insured against accidents becase they want to keep it secret. But theowner of the ship, that tight fella, could not bear not insuringthem in secret, so the insurancecompany hired the Radzeer. So the condition was that we had to follow the André Deremio and the tourists on. These turists were all marqees, lorts, shareowners, factory directors and other magnates and they took it into their heads that they wanted to imitate a certain Cruzoe, who lived alone in a deserted book. On a completelly lonelly island and withouth anything, he just had a servant and complete equipment. It was said that he was called Rotbinzon Cruso. His servant was a 'Saturday' local. They had to be sick people, because if one has somuch mony to furnish an entire island and the person is not on the beach in Miammi or go to Losange-Ales to hang with filmstars, he's a big donkey, so it is better if he gets himself seen by a doc tor.

But tourists are like that.

Once they climb up to the mountain ice to the glacciers, then sit on camels and get malaria, becase they have to see how the mumies buried in the piramids are lying, boxed up real egyptians. These are your royal colleages, ruling under the name of parao. (The pointy tablets named piramids that were used as graves, are found in the desert by excavation.) So it was that these tourists went on Deremit Andrie to be Rotbinzons, but not just one servant called 'Saturday', but so many serving chaps that they could be named after the entire calendar. From Monday to Happy New Year. And they took every commonly needed things, so that they could spend a year on the deserted island. It is grisly dangerous over there because it is the home of coral and atoll. According to superstitious sailors the coral and the atoll grows all the time and their sons of stone branch out under the water. It is said that this is why one can not find an island because it wilted under the water in the mean time. And finds a new one, which wilts up from under the water suddenly.

The Inconbnito Archipell is such an island surrounded by atoll reef.

To get back to the subject, as the insurance company ordered the following of the ship, the Radzeer was sneaking behind the Remio André De a day apart, so the other did not suspect the destination. We were such fine sailors that this sneaking was so successful that even the insurance company did not guess our destinations. Tis is good service. Becase we wondered if we could make any other business there.

When the tourist ship left Kap Blumt by a few degrees a world miracle happened! We just discovered it as the Professor was looking into telescopic. Then he dropped the telescope... As if he went gaga... Then he shouted into the tube of the ship bridge: "Stop! Half right!... Even my old grandfather did not see anything like this! Half steam!"

And he was right with the commandeering! Becase one's honourable lineage, old mugger grandfather could be as well travelled as Rotbinzon Cruze, he would never have seen anything like this! Your highness' eyes would have stared out of his head like a fried fish.

Becase what was this vision? Too bad even for a dream!

This moron Rotbinzon ship, was standing in the distance in the middle of a mile wide island. But right in!

Everyone thought that they went mad and eyes played trick.

Your Highness knows that I am not superstitious and I not care a hoot about magic, becase in Lima the inca high priest gave me an amulet against such things. But even I throw a cross.

Us old sea wolves looked at it puzzled from afar. 1 smoking ship in the middle of 1 piece of large land. At night so that the steamer did not see us we approached the island in darkness. It was the Incognit Archipel where those nasty tourists headed. The ship was stranded in the middle of a piece of land sticking out of the main island, slightly listed to the left, half in the mud.

And the mistery was solved!

Tis was a stupid case that happened maybe once in 5 thusand years. We saw that the land piece was full of such enormous water plants was called moss and grass, and all sorts of sea creatures were still swarming on it like snakes, polip and even squid. So this was a seabed not long ago! And the whole thing was made of a strange narrow pink knitted rock! This was the living creation atolrock that developed itself under water. So what does your majesty think in your head what happened?

Towards the island this Andrémie De slowed down and suddenly this reef, just as the ship was above it, rose from the water!

Tis atols reef, was the continuation of the shore, and under the water! The ship suddenly saw that it was retrained as a train because it was going in the middle of a little island! At tis of course leaned sideway, burrowed the nose into the sludge but as it was going at barely steam it did not turn over.

Was it not a miracle?

Tat a ship had such stupid luck with a reef? Tat it was going above it at the time when it was coming up?

It was evening and in the distance moon they were very visible but we not.

They did not need urgent help because on dry land a ship doesn't sink. So we started to look at the world miracle from a business angle.

"This is all big lords", said the Professor, "and the ransom is beautiful if they were hijacked."

"We cannot hijack them", panted Fat Petters, "becase they were insured with us against us. And robber here or there, there's either honour or not!"

We thought for long. The Busi Weasel was blinking with his wire eyes called pincenez (but looking above it) as if he was cooking something in his head. And on that head that black wide felt hat, and under the long hanging grey hairdo, the warty old face covered a lot of brain.

We waited to hear what plan of his popped out.

"But", he said then and his really enormous nose was moving like when he's sniffing business, "what if we also ran aground? Tis really was possible with an unlucky reef! And canot be considered dishonourable. Sea was like this: dangerous and every trip was rugged on it."

"Don't twist the words here!", said the Moonlight Charli. "Spit out what you think!"

"Simple", said Weasel. "A great reward will be offered for both ships. And then we will find ourselfes. Someone goes back to seeker."

"But we didn't run aground", said Spikey Vanek sadly, with whom anno detto your highness scuffled with intimately.

"If you let me at the wheel", said this Busi Weasel, "I will run aground so, accidently, tat we wouldn't even be standing so stupidly like these. But first comes this Smiley Jimmi (tat was me), he was taken on the last day, so nobody knows he is on the ship. So first we turn back, drop him off at Marquesas and we come back. If we don't pay attention we run aground. Why pay attention all the time anyway? Then there will be a lot of reward money. Smiley Jimmy will come for us and finds us."

This plan met with the middle of universal agreement.

The discussion result was ready. Radzeer will take me near Marquesas island. There I go ashore in a rowboat get to Tahiti on a steamer and then Frisco. In the meantime the Radzeer will tiptoe back and runs aground so skilfully on that island tongue as if it was stuck out suddenly.

The radio of the Deremi Andréo steamer was done in the collision, so the Radzeer did not send signals either. And decided that if our ship stands in the reef as scheduled, they will also waste the ship's radio. They will lean a tree trunk against the mast as if this was a result of the catastrophe as well.

Everything went as per plan. But in Oakland fate's strange cruelness brought me together with a man named after certain Dirty Manfred captain that I mentioned before – I think from an earlier dated.

And this one is always stirring it!

First I decided that I would divert our chivalry business into the trail of knifing, but later I didn't do it in the end. Old person, so let him live. Your Highnes knows my soft heart. But what a coincidence! The captain named after him got an assignment from the directorate of the English consulate to lead an ekspedition against the unlucky ones. But he said that if the devil took his fellows, with the Radzeer, it would be a shame to find them. (This isn't a half-friend saying, but he really is not a half-friend but unfriendly.)

So then I was hired. But this Dirt Alfred, stirred it that I had to team up with the bluebeard person. Only this way could the Blind Dad be mine. (Your highness this is such a title that you could not consider it an insult and in any case it doesn't mean a blind parent but a ship.)

But what a splendid one!

And it then came out that not only this bluebeard is my partner in the ekspedition but someone else too.

I don't like involving such fink people in regular swindles but I had to do it for the Blind Dad.

I will continue to date the further development of the case with my new fountain pen, from Marcuasas and accept my returned royal remembering for your loyalty. I remain by my own dated below

Bye until write again,

Don Smiley di St James m.p.

P.S. I don't know of your kingship heard of the Bluebeard? He is a well know chap and if you interested I will write about him separate. Just ask you again to stay silent about the case with discreet lordliness your highness.

Smiley as above

Chapter Nine

When Smiley Jimmy finally found Pirate Pepi in the Three Red Corkscrews, a new period of his life started. This pirate was surprisingly pretty! She looked like a porcelain figurine with smooth black hair, which was a result of taming her unruly headdress with oil. She was wearing a chequered dress, but it seemed that the tailor miscalculated the material because the dress stretched over her figure so tightly that it almost creaked when she walked. One expected that the dress would just slide upwards all the way any second. But Pirate Pepi was not afraid of this.

Actually she wasn't afraid of anything.

On the split of the neckline some scraggy, narrow fur decoration hung, and she carried an enormous leather handbag, hooked over her lower arm. Her beautiful features were vulgarised by cheap powder and overly bright lips. Somehow though, this made her even prettier. She was wearing a saucy little hat made for a bun, put sideways on her head, and she walked energetically through the inn, the men involuntarily giving way to her two marching arms. Many pieces of jewellery rattled on her wrists: pearls, wristlets, and even an unlikely large brooch decorated with gemstones. Colourful and plain glass sparkled on her fingers, and needless to say perhaps that Pirate Pepi's jewellery represented not a single carat to a jeweller's eyes.

That is, if a jeweller's eyes would even waste a glimpse on such articles.

"Are you that Smiley Jimmy who wanted to speak to me to become partners?", she said, and she sat down forcefully, shaking back her bracelets. "So you can come on board, I don't mind, but I'm warning you that you must behave yourself. Hey!... Jack! Whisky, half a glass, from the dollar one!"

She put a cigarette bent in half in her mount from the top pocket of her dress and flicked her lighter.

The devil! What a woman!

"Look, ladyship…"

"I am Pirate Pepi."

"Listen, Miss Pirate. The thing is that I was assigned this case, for fifty thousand dollars. I am Captain Smiley Jimmy, you must have heard this name before."

"Not yet", said the woman, and she downed the half a glass of whisky in one gulp. "But I remember one of your relatives mentioned before. A certain similarly-named quartermaster. Are you brothers?"

"Hmm… I was a quartermaster as well before. But that's not the main thing. I believe we will get along very well."

"If not, I don't care anyway. So you will bear all the costs, for your third of the reward?"

"What?!", he snorted angrily. "Wagner and you will get half and I will get half?!"

"I don't have much time. And I'm not interested in foolishness. It will be split into three equal shares, if you don't like it, you can find another ship…"

The ground should swallow this captain! But what could he do? He had to accept everything. As soon as they agreed in principle, Pirate Pepi opened her enormous handbag, which was stuffed with all sorts of things. Amongst others a set of pliers and a six-shooter revolver was to be found there, and a colourful silk handkerchief next to her compact. After a long search she pulled out a wrinkled sheet of paper and she smoothed it out. It was a ready-prepared contract. Smiley Jimmy signed it with a big sigh.

"Now you must go and find a crew, and I will search as well", said Pirate Pepi. "We will wait for each other by the old dock."

"But one must be careful here…"

"Don't you try teaching me! I will not bring anyone shabbier than you."

Smiley Jimmy looked after her, as she rushed off with her muscles squirming under her dress. It was true that 'what a woman!', but it would have been pleasant to deal a blow sometimes when he opened his mouth so stupidly wide.

He went back to the Three-Mast Soda. It was hardly child's play to find a crew at the height of the season and especially for a trip like this.

Nobody signed up readily to a ship that sailed beyond Cape Blount to search for the steamers that mysteriously disappeared in the Incognita Islands.

"Hey, Jimmy!", shouted someone croakily, and as he turned around he saw Red Vasich, who was drunk again as usual. His old friend wanted to throw himself on his neck with open arms but he missed and fell to the ground.

Jimmy helped him up happily. This one was an outstanding mechanic! He could also steer, even if not in the home of the coral and atoll reefs.

"You Vasich! Will you sign up with me?"

"But of course!"

"We are going to Cape Blount, after the Radzeer."

Red, although staggering and with eyeballs shining like pearls, appeared after a short consideration to have changed his mind.

"You know, there is something…"

"All right, all right", waved Smiley Jimmy, who was clear about the difficulty of this method of verbal recruitment. "I didn't count on you anyway, I need all grown-ups for this, notorious dock lads…"

According to experienced police inspectors, there was hardly a more notorious lad than Red Vasich in the registry of individuals with no papers and always at sea. On top of that Vasich was quite short of stature, so the 'not grown-up' comment hit home particularly.

"Say that one more time and I shall smash your face in!", he replied and tugged hard at his belt, which slipped from his hand and he hit a passer-by in the stomach with his elbow instead.

"It's pointless to fight right now", said Smiley Jimmy, "I have to hurry to find some useful lads."

"Well now, here I am for one! Nobody can mouth off about me saying that I wasn't into something that needed a real man."

Here was a first class acquisition. For whatever reason, here and there lonely, long pieces of hair grew on his alcoholism-induced puffed up, reddish, round face. The hair had to be avoided by the barber as well during shaving so that they didn't grow too much. Some years ago he had stolen a straw hat on some beach which was used by ladies as a sunshade, this is what he wore. He was a middle-built, tubby, shabby-looking individual, with a swollen, wide mouth, and for some reason or other he was always scratching himself. One who did not know him wouldn't have allowed him on his ship even if he had paid for it.

But anyone who knew the real value of a sailor would understand Knot Bill's cocky, misanthropically arrogant behaviour that he displayed in all situations. This behaviour did not change even when a ship was sinking, or when he carried out his duties in a cyclone.

"Hello Bill!", Jimmy greeted him.

"Hi!", he replied. "It would be quite urgent for me to get away from here, I was finked on by someone for some reason. Do you happen to know a ship?"

"A first class one! The Blind Dad! We're leaving immediately!"

"Immediately I cannot do. I have some small business to attend to at the Pharaoh."

The Pharaoh was the inn of an Egyptian owner, in the darkest alleyways of the old town; it was the meeting place of the darkest individuals.

"We'll go with you and wait for you to finish", said Smiley Jimmy.

"And if it's about slaps... we'll even help", said the Red Vasich in between two hiccups. He was right, it was precisely about slaps.

"The main thing is", explained Knot Bill on the way, "that I want to break that wretched pub into smithereens. I must get people to lose the habit of finking on me", he explained in his throaty, drawn-out voice.

"We'll put things right!", nodded Smiley Jimmy. "The main thing is to sort it out quickly because we need to meet with Pirate Pepi soon."

He saw somewhat reassuringly that there were only ten or twelve people in the room and the turbaned, fat Egyptian owner was sitting behind the counter. When Knot Bill stepped in, he was thrown a bottle at without further ado, which missed him by a hair.

As a reply Vasich threw an entire table and a chair immediately at the group, and the fat Egyptian, who jumped over the shelves with a kitchen knife, was thrown out into the street by Smiley Jimmy in such a way that his return was highly doubtful.

Knot Bill worked frighteningly. He smashed the liquor stand with one of the guys, than he jumped straight at the people coming at him so that they spun about and when they turned around a half-meter wide mirror fell on them. In the meantime Smiley Jimmy and Vasich took care of the rest of the furniture with their attack.

"Wait!", panted Knot Bill.

With a readily held red marl piece he wrote onto the wall with large, awkward letters:

This is where Knot Bill was finked on.
And the owner was in on it.
Good Bye!

The crowd outside was staring at them, but according to the rules in the suburbs if someone had no business in the case he should not interfere. And even if someone felt like interfering, the feeling would have passed at the sight of these three infamous lads, who now rushed off towards the docks.

Following Knot Bill's directions, they found Shirker Hugo. That was good. But there was no steersman. The one available was not worth a penny. Luckily they got hold of a boatswain. His skeleton-like sticking out ribs, his dominant wide shoulders, pointy elbows and his general skinniness earned him the name of the Bone Toff. And still no steersman. Towards midnight Pirate Pepi arrived with a first class crew. She chose them well, because amongst them was the outstanding person of Swedish Ox, and Stripy Harry, an excellent radioman. He received the title 'Stripy' because of his cut up face. The rest was also good material.

"But there is no steersman", shouted Pirate Pepi, and she slapped her thigh so that the sound echoed through the entire neighbourhood.

"And we don't want anyone from the agency...", muttered Jimmy.

"I will drive that buggy..."

They all turned around. A strange, strikingly handsome individual stood nearby leaning against a lamp post. He had just finished rolling up, he wetted the cigarette paper, pulled the match over his trousers and lit up.

"Where the hell did this one come from?", wondered Pirate Pepi.

"The Copper Baron!", said Smiley Jimmy with a reserved enthusiasm. After all, he was not happy when such a handsome dandy stood in the way of his ambition. Because the Copper Baron was a famous pretty boy in the docks. And being Spanish (he claimed to be Spanish) he knew about picturesque elegance. His unruly, curly, red hair, his bronze, interesting face, his pretty flashy, blue or red neckties, colourful chequered or yellow silk shirts, rigid, wide shoes, fine deerskin trousers, wide big-buckled belt, and last but not least his muscular, slim figure was all a stick in Smiley Jimmy's throat. On top of that he sang splendidly, he played the guitar, when he laughed the sparkle of his pearl-white row of teeth competed with the deep heat of his gaze and any woman who would not fall at his feet at first sight would have a heart of stone. Not to mention that he was a captain, steersman, mechanic and boatswain before, first class at all of them.

"You would come along?...", asked Smiley Jimmy moodily.

"So I said."

And he already smiled at Pirate Pepi so that his face melted into an amiable, cheeky wrinkle. But that one was not made of butter either.

"Are you a good steersman?"

"Don't make yourself ridiculous, Pepi", commented Shirker Hugo. "This one brought back the Hurricane from the Arctic, with a broken compass."

"In that case come with us. I am Pirate Pepi... Hey! Do you want to bite my hand?"

The 'captain' jerked her hand away, but she blushed.

...The next morning, when they had finished loading, the Blind Dad pulled up the anchor and headed south under full steam.

Her voyage, although perhaps the sailors on board were not aware of it, was accompanied with great expectation and concern from individuals in very high places.

She sent a radio message to the admiral's office from Samoa, than Fiji, and reported triumphantly that they had sailed past Cape Blount by a few degrees.

A few days went by... Hundreds and hundreds of radios were waiting for a signal from the Blind Dad... To no avail!

The steamer sent no sign of life from beyond Cape Blount. A third ship had disappeared on this mysterious part of the ocean...

Chapter Ten

After they departed, peace was broken by a few flashes of show of power. The avalanche was set off by Mr Wagner. The rum he drank was either not enough or did not have a high enough alcohol content; what was certain was that at departure he appeared on the bridge swaying less than usual. He pulled out something from his inside pocket, so that several lock picks, faded flowers and a piece of roast pumpkin also fell onto the deck. Then he put that something on his head and it turned out that he used the volunteer police force's hat as a captain's hat. He then shouted into the speaking tube confidently, soldierly:

"What's up, fellas? Is there no steam in this strovacheck?! Or are you slacking here?!"

Just then Smiley Jimmy appeared on the bridge and notified the Bluebeard that if he didn't go to the hold immediately he would chuck him into the sea.

"But my dear strovacheck!... I am Dirty Fred's adjutant... You just need to take a look at me!... All these rascals know me well..."

Smiley Jimmy discreetly threw Mr Wagner into the second steersman's empty cabin so that the door fell in with him. Now the Copper Baron stopped under the bridge and shouted up:

"Hey, you! My captain is Wagner. I like him better than you."

Smiley Jimmy rushed down to him.

"Since when do you appoint captains?!"

"Look, Smiley Jimmy", he said, and he adjusted his belt with the splendid buckle. "It's high time that we exchange a few honest punches between us."

"I am of that opinion as well. Because I think you are just a braggart."

"Enough at least to choose wisely who I name captain. It's not a question of leather gaiters you know."

This hit home!

Smiley Jimmy respected his leather gaiters like some house idol. It was part of his personality that if something hit home he rarely missed the jawline as a reply.

He struck the Copper Baron.

Thwack!

Bang, pop!

There was a big fight... The steersman fell into the kitchen, and the cook into the food. But he was up already... He fell back again from a kick and he jumped up so that he could deliver his famous straight left, which made Smiley Jimmy simply fly off as if he was practicing gliding without the wings. He got tangled up in Shirker Hugo's pile of ropes and he received a minimum of sixteen slaps from the Copper Baron (each was a prime specimen) by the time he managed to get himself untangled.

And after he got untangled, a hook sent him to the floor again, but with a devilish speciality he also knocked the Copper Baron off his feet in his fall and they fell on top of each other. They jumped up at the same time and the four heavy fists were falling again.

Bang, pop!

Bank, pop, thwack!

The boys stood around goggling.

This was a rare good fight! It was not every day that the people of the docks saw one of these when two fighters stood and landed a shower of punches. Such big ones that a person with looser bone structure would have his skull split into shreds from half of them. The Copper Baron's right hand held Smiley Jimmy by the throat against the air funnel, but that terrible slap he received in return, so that his blood sprayed everywhere, was not negligible either. In reply he smashed the frigate lieutenant's head against the air funnel so that it resounded and bent (not the head but the funnel), but in the meantime he received two slaps with the power of a sweeping monsoon, then a kick reached the knee area... They fell on top of each other! Rolling on the ground they pounded each other, whoever happened to be on top. They were handing out gruesome punches, grabbing each other's hair with a spare hand and the deck resounded from the heads being hit against it...

Bumm!

A shot was fired and a sharp shrill split the air:

"Hands up!"

The shouting would not have been enough, but the shot made them jump to their feet instinctively. Pirate Pepi stood there, with her open handbag over her arm, the six-shooter was still smoking in her hand.

"What is this!", she shouted in her energetic, deep voice, and even her dress stretched unusually in her attack stance. "What's this? Refusal of service at sea? Be careful! I know the regulations. Anyone who causes trouble on the ship I will bump off like blazes!"

The two men were only somewhat recognisable from their clothing. But neither of them was even panting. They were patting their black and blue, sore, swollen faces and grumbling.

"You did not tell me", shouted the Copper Baron angrily to Pirate Pepi, "that this one would be captain here."

"I had the right to shoot him on the spot!", replied Smiley Jimmy. "The steersman revolted against me and…"

"Shut up!"

This was what Pirate Pepi said curtly and quietly, then lit a cigarette and walked up to the bridge. There the third culprit, Mr Wagner, was snoozing peacefully. In his police hat!

"Excuse me…", said Mr Wagner to the woman, with the broken cabin door under his arm. "Does your ladyship know by any chance where this ship is headed?"

He fell backwards with door in hand from a brief, dismissive wave of a hand, then flew off the bridge. Pirate Pepi slapped her chest again and gave a brief speech:

"I am the captain! Smiley Jimmy is the first officer and the Copper Baron is the steersman! If anyone doesn't like this, report now!... And now everyone go to your business and the one who starts a fight I will bump off like…"

"…. like blazes! We've heard that already…", muttered Smiley Jimmy and rushed off.

"We'll continue this somewhere else!", whispered the Copper Baron next to him.

"I hope I won't have to wait a year again for it", replied Smiley Jimmy with a savage look. "And it's better if you leave Pirate Pepi alone. She doesn't fall for colourfully clothed toffs like you."

"Then why are you concerned whether I leave her alone or not?"

They were measuring each other up for a few seconds, but orders were shouted from the bridge and the two angry men went to do their work.

"This one has a pretty good idea of the job", whispered Bone Toff, the boatswain, to Shirker Hugo, and pointed his head towards the captain. They were not interested in the business of the first officer and the steersman. That was a done deal. Sooner or later one of them will put the other one cold. On the other hand Pirate Pepi, the captain, was a great surprise. She knew her job very well. She commanded the Blind Dad so skilfully that even the old sea bears could not have done it better. Before they reached port, the Swedish Ox wanted to hurry up to the bridge to help with the navigation, because he feared that their new captain may smash a few barges or run up the shore.

"What do you want here? Go to your work!", shouted Pirate Pepi, then she gave out short, firm orders and everything went so smoothly that they just stood there with their mouths open…

She carried out her patrols before midnight precisely and regularly. She noticed the smallest of errors and often stopped to speak to people while smoking a cigarette.

"Where did you learn to sail like this?", asked Shirker Hugo when she stopped during her patrol at the entrance of between-decks.

"My dad served for forty years on the Baltimore", she replied and sat down amongst them on the stairs; she took out a saggy cigarette and stuck it in the corner of her mouth. "He was a cabin boy there, then a sailor, and for twenty years as a captain. When my mother died, he had no choice but to take me along with him and I grew up there, on the Baltimore."

There was a squeaking sound as the ship tilted slightly, and Pirate Pepi turned around because she knew that Smiley Jimmy was looking at her from somewhere in the shadows.

"An excellent story", said the frigate lieutenant.

"That's true", said Pirate Pepi and jumped up, "but it would be even more excellent if someone oiled the pulleys so that they don't squeal so much."

Smiley Jimmy wanted to accompany her on her patrol but Pirate Pepi informed him that there was no need for that. Woe betide any dock hooligan who dared go near this woman when she was 'working'. They took this very seriously.

Only when Pirate Pepi had checked every corner of the Blind Dad, did she return to her cabin.

Her attention spread over everything on the way. Perhaps more so than her duty would have demanded, because she checked in on the steering room twice. First the Copper Baron informed her that everything was in order, later he cheekily grinned when he said:

"Everything is still in order."

"I didn't ask what's up!", shouted back Pirate Pepi anxiously. "But you cannot stand by the wheel day and night."

"Smiley Jimmy can relieve me here, but once we reach Cape Blount I would need to sleep here in the steering room and preferably steer continuously because nobody can take the ship there apart from me... Unless...", and he grinned, "the captain knows the South Seas through and through."

The captain took out a saggy cigarette which needed to be wetted with her lips here and there before she could light it and replied:

"Why are you so insolent with me all the time?"

She asked this more curiously than annoyed.

"I have an unfortunate nature like that", he replied with a pharisaic expression, sighing deeply.

The captain looked him up and down, with undisguised contempt.

"One day when we quarrel about something you will not talk to me like you do with one of the female acquaintance from the ball room."

"That can easily happen", he nodded, but not changing his tooth-flashing, impertinent grin.

The captain rushed off annoyed, and at midnight she handed over her duties to Smiley Jimmy. The voyage seemed relatively smooth and still…

When they got closer to Cape Blount, a certain nervousness spread amongst the crew. After all, they were sailing on seas where two ships had passed before them and disappeared without sending a single radio signal. The battleship practising around the Marquesas and the Swallow heading to Tasmania insisted back then that they should have definitely intercepted a transmission if either of the ships had sent distress signals. How could they sink, what sort of catastrophe could have happened to both ships that they did not even have time to send a distress signal?

It was obvious that there was only one way. If they got into a big storm and they could not reduce the fire enough and somehow the water got into the boiler, the ship would have turned into one single enormous hand grenade and been blown into smithereens before the radio operator even had an idea what was going on. But there was no storm detected at that time from the South Pole to the archipelago, and the meteorologists knew everything precisely.

None of them said it but they were all of the same opinion that there were only two possibilities: either natives attacked their ship at night near an island where they made port, or, and this was a more plausible hypothesis, The Green Bloke's bony hand was at work. Because the sea beyond Cape Blount, all the way to the South Pole, was the Green Bloke's eternal country. As they were sitting on the steps, Knot Bill carried the conversation. Knot Bill was an interesting person, as his name showed.

He was always chewing on a cigar end but this was almost never lit, and he carried a whisky flask in his back pocket. It was a particular characteristic of his that he liked sweet alcohol. It was unusual because normally in dock circles sweet drinks were ordered for ladies.

Knot Bill on the other hand liked sweet drinks and whether on duty or not, in destructive hurricane or calm, he pulled out his flask filled with sweet liquor periodically from his back pocket.

One of his captains observed that he took a sip almost automatically, with the preciseness of a clock, after every knot travelled. Since then he had been called Knot Bill.

"In my opinion", he said thoughtfully to those sitting around him, because he knew that his general knowledge was well respected, "there must have been some disagreement between the Green Bloke and the Radzeer for some time now. This happened at the time when Dirty Fred and this moron Bluebeard allegedly manipulated with the Radzeer and the plague-stricken Brigit at the same time, and it is said that the Captain, being such a dog when money is in question, foxed the Green Bloke."

They were silent. The ship was sailing in dead calm, and soft, independent clouds of fog started to appear. From somewhere waves arrived and slightly tilted the Blind Dad with a soft push.

Knot Bill took out his sweet filled flask and drank. With long, measured sips. They all remembered the Brigit's murky business, and they were susceptible to assume about the Captain that he would even fox the Green Bloke with his sharp brain. For a while, when they arrived back at Frisco, the Professor and Fat Petters and the other sailors of the Radzeer were throwing money around just like nothing. If there was money in question, this mingy-hearted Dirty Fred would even fox Satan himself.

"But that time Smiley Jimmy and the Copper Baron were also on the Radzeer!", said Bone Toff.

"That's true. But I don't recommend that you enquire from them without an open penknife. Because the Radzeer is usually making such trips that a big silence follows after each one. And the crew has more than enough money and if someone enquires too much, they catch him in a dark corner of the docks and he is no more! No more curiosity."

"But after all", murmured the Swedish Ox, "we had no business on the Green Bloke's sea. For that…"

"For what?", replied Knot Bill angrily. "Here is Smiley Jimmy and the Copper Baron. I say if a ship sinks on the Green Bloke's sea, or nobody knows what happened to it, and there were no radio transmissions either, it is best to go back empty handed. Believe me."

"Why didn't you say this before?!"

"Because", replied Knot Bill, "it was so urgent for me to leave Frisco that I didn't care about anything. If you want to know, Red Vasich was also part of the Radzeer's business when that chivalrous case happened with the Green Bloke…"

"The whole case was", said someone unexpectedly from above them, "that my good old friend, the great Man of the Dirty and me, received a business offer from a female-name

75

ship!... Yes, yes, my friends, this female-name ship, if I remember right the Belladonna, this was loading plague somewhere and businessmen were sought to go on board and burn her! In the open ocean! Hullo! The open sea is the most beautiful in the world."

Following this speech Mr Wagner slid down rolling over about six steps, along with the door that he carried with him.

"One question", said Knot Bill, "how did the plague-ship Brigit get into this business?"

"I will tell that as well, my dear friend! I think for twenty dollars! But no! Twenty such money that is paid in Egypt and is still English... We sank this ship with the Captain, and she later resurrected, and sank again, and in the end everyone ran away. It is best if all of us now sing the entrance of the Ace of Clubs from the opera Lohengrin..."

But before he could turn to aria, true to his habit, he suddenly fell asleep. The cabin door under his head. Knot Bill took out his flask and drank, which notified everyone that they could not have reached the southern stream because they could not have travelled more than a knot during that time.

They were sitting there solemn, silent.

Smiley Jimmy, who took over duty earlier, from time to time returned to the captain's cabin on his round, and was standing there deep in thought. He would have been greatly surprised to see that Pirate Pepi's harsh, slighting face strangely smoothed out when she was alone and did not see the need to make an impression on the ragged man on the ship.

She was writing something into a small notebook, and she was making tea. Smiley Jimmy could not see this, because the window of the captain's cabin was two meters high above him. But light was seeping out at the corner of the door.

Smiley Jimmy, when passing by the door for the third time, finally knocked.

"Yes!", shouted a calm, sonorous voice from inside. The frigate lieutenant tugged at his jacket, straightened his collar and stepped inside.

"Good evening!", he said, and he tried to greet the captain with his widest, most pleasant smile.

"Good evening!", replied this one calmly. "Is something the matter?"

"Not really. We should just discuss… the ship's business… from the point of view…"

"I don't like discussions at night. In any case, what point of view I should be discussing with you?"

The captain's voice was not stern and still… Smiley Jimmy felt as if he was doused by cold water. What a conceited woman!

"Just from the point… I mean to discuss, that here on the ship as I heard earlier by chance… the crew is talking all sorts of nonsense, which could cause trouble. They're mentioning this Green Bloke, and that drunken Wagner is driving them on…"

"This is important business. And we will discuss it tomorrow. Good night!"

When Smiley Jimmy left, feeling slightly scalded, immediately next to him, on the dark deck, someone started quietly laughing from behind a cigarette's embers. The Copper Baron stood there.

"I see that you strayed into the captain's cabin during your rounds…"

"So what! Why do you need to snigger about it?", he asked with puffed up chest as usual.

"Not so fast, Jimmy! It seems that the captainship got into your head."

The frigate lieutenant swallowed bitterly… The devil take all these godforsaken tramps. They were always bothered about him being captain. Why were they not bothered about Rugged Morton or Breeches? They were dock lads just the same as him. But still, as soon as they heard that Smiley Jimmy was first officer or captain, this riff-raff started to mouth off about it straight away. This was not the first time. But those punches he handed to the Copper Baron were not the first ones either for a similar occasion. Although this was not skimpy… And now he was boiling one's blood even more, this determined cock. They stood in front of each other, their jackets touching. The Copper Baron's cigarette lit up mockingly in front of his face.

"You have nothing to do with my captainship."

"Leave this woman, Jimmy", said the steersman quietly. "She's not for you."

"Perhaps she's falling for you then?"

"I didn't say that", said the other indifferently. And he added wonderingly: "But it's possible…"

"This?", laughed Smiley Jimmy nervously and mockingly. "This one doesn't give a damn about blokes like you. She does not look the type that cares about a man in silk rags and gaudy things."

The other one nodded slowly:

"I see. So she's mad about leather gaiters… Oho!"

…He suddenly grabbed Smiley Jimmy's surging wrist. But it was not the iron grab that held the enormous hand back, but a calm voice:

"It's not well done, Jimmy. We are now in the South Seas and if we do each other in, the whole company will spend the weekend under water the day after tomorrow. Because there is no-one able to take our places."

This was true. To hell with economy. There was not a spare one to replace any of them. And this Swedish Ox or Shirker Hugo and Vasich, they're tough in their own rights, they could even steer but not beyond Cape Blount.

"What's true is true!", nodded therefore Smiley Jimmy with a sigh. "But don't forget our rendezvous in Frisco."

"Is someone telling stories about me being forgetful?", replied the other with a frozen smile.

They were silent... Underneath them the ship's old heart grumbled, pulsated, squeaked restlessly. Smiley Jimmy wandered off to continue his rounds on the narrow spiral staircase, down to the engine room. The Copper Baron looked around, than with cat-like steps sneaked over to the captain's cabin in the dark.

The deck was deserted. The rustling sound of water streaming around the ship was clearly audible. He tied a rope around his waist to leave a long tail, he tied a grapple-iron to this and hurried up the chimney's metal ladder. The cabin window that he wished to spy through was above human height. If he stepped on top of the cabin however, Pirate Pepi would hear the sound of his footsteps. This was why he came up with this neck-breaking idea of snooping. He hooked the iron into a step, pushed himself away and swinging like a pendulum, with small movements, at every other second his face reached the round window. The Copper Baron was not snooping around out of mere curiosity. He belonged to that group of selected military personnel who acted for the Secret Service: his real name was Milton Winter and he was a corvette captain.

He was surprised to see that Pirate Pepi's cabin was empty. Where could this woman be?

"I am here!", replied an energetic, sonorous voice behind and under him.

The steersman turned around in his suspended state in alarm, and he saw Pirate Pepi there, naturally with her enormous six-shooter in her hand.

This was a delicate situation indeed! The Copper Baron was hanging there with a humble, polite pose and he attempted to smile amiably.

"Good evening, Pirate Pepi", he said in his awkward situation with a pleasant smile that made his face distorted. "Where have you been that I couldn't see you in your cabin?"

"What are you doing up there?"

"A little exercise is beneficial after work!", he flapped around politely. "In any case I wanted to call on you in your cabin... Miss Pepi!", and he pressed his hand to his heart, with this he almost brushed himself away in his unstable situation, "I love you!"

"Really?", replied the woman coldly. "That's sweet. According to the sayings of my home country a hung man's love confession brings luck."

"I am happy that you..."

"Enough!". She stamped her feet forcefully and lifted her revolver, squinting slightly with her right eye. "Well?! Come on!"

The steersman obeyed. He swung to the ladder, unhooked the iron, then rushed to Pirate Pepi on the deck and with a real Spanish grandiosity he sunk to half a knee:

"Mia bella senorita! I adore you!"

Pirate Pepi recoiled a bit. It seemed that this confession had a great effect on her. But this proved to be misleading as the next second the Copper Baron received such a slap from his lady of heart that Shirker Hugo rushed to the stern because he thought that the plummet was torn off and that's what made that loud splashing sound in the night.

"Strike me dead, senorita!", continued the steersman dauntlessly. "To die for love, carramba!... That's a real gentlemanly fate, my father was a Spanish hidalgo from Old Castilia!"

"Strange", marvelled Pirate Pepi. "As far as I know, a foreign national cannot be an officer in England for the navy. How did the descendant of Milton hidalgo Winter manage to become a corvette captain?"

The Copper Baron's face muscles jerked. Pirate Pepi knew his secret! This woman therefore had to be a spy or the agent of some international intelligence bureau.

The steersman's love confession was not entirely an act, but his obligation to fulfil his duty to England stood above all other interests. This woman had to die!

"I see", he said in an unchanged happy tone, "that Miss Pepi must have had a lot to drink tonight to mix me up with someone else, even though she saw my papers…"

"Yes!", laughed the woman nervously. "While you were asleep, I saw your papers!" And she quickly pulled out the corvette captain's secret service ID. "Here are your papers and…"

At this moment the ground was taken from underneath her, she fell over the deck at full length and felt that the revolver was torn from her hand.

She did not notice in the dark that the kneeling Copper Baron's hands slowly reached out, grabbed her ankles and plop... he threw himself on her! After that Pirate Pepi could only feel that the scream building in her throat was supressed by a strong male hand pressed over her mouth, she was raised in the air and her frightened eyes spotted the deep splashing waves above the rails.

Pirate Pepi knew that there was no mercy, and the next moment she would fly...

Why did this officer hesitate? What sort of passion was fighting with his sense of duty and winning? Passion usually found the perfect excuse against duty: he had to search the woman's pockets. It was important to know who this mysterious person was. These were the sort of things he said to himself while he stood her back on her feet.

"Psst... If you utter a single sound I will throw you overboard..."

Pirate Pepi stood motionless because the steersman's hands were permanently placed firmly on her neck, although without applying pressure. She knew that only a miracle could help her now.

For a moment the moon appeared from behind the frilly edge of a cloud and shone briefly over the sullen surface of the ocean... Lazy, large waves rolled towards the ship. An unoiled pulley squeaked near them...

The woman wanted to shout but she did not dare. She was breathing heavily...

And in this hopeless, fatal situation a miracle came to her aid! A wonderful fortune! A soft step sounded next to them... As if he came from the floor planks, suddenly Smiley Jimmy appeared! A step away from them. The Copper Baron let go of Pirate Pepi and grabbed the revolver in his pocket.

For a second this picture was frozen amongst the rest of the shadows of the night: they did not move. Only the sound of

Smiley Jimmy's heavy breathing was heard, as he inflated his chest like a fighting cock.

The three of them stood there, invisible electricity between them, the sudden silence was so static.

"Someone appeared to have screamed", Smiley Jimmy said quietly, looking from one to the other with a searching gaze.

A pause. The wind got hold of a half loose canvas cover and was flapping it like the wing of an enormous trapped bat. Now a really surprising thing happened. The Copper Baron would not have been more surprised if the chimney started to speak, it was so stunningly strange. Pirate Pepi turned to Smiley Jimmy and coldly, calmly, said this:

"Of course you heard a scream, I've asked a hundred times to have that wretched back light pulley oiled. But it's no use to say anything here!"

And as the ship tilted slightly in the slow waves, the unoiled pulley's squeak sounded again...

Smiley Jimmy stood there for a second, feeling scolded. He looked them over once more with sad eyes burning with fight, then slowly walked away.

They stood there together. They remained motionless. The Copper Baron so stupidly that even his mouth dropped open in his surprise. This woman saved him, and made nothing of the fact that he attacked her ready to kill? Or what?...

"Well then!... What are you waiting for?...", shouted Pirate Pepi. "Or are you not going to throw me into the water?"

"What's this?!...", said the Copper Baron hoarsely. "You... you... let me go?! Answer me, please!", he finished almost rudely and grabbed the woman's wrist.

"Come to my cabin!", said the captain with a sweet smile and she pulled her wrist away with ease. "You may drink a cup of tea with me, you... you murderer!"

Chapter Eleven

Milton was returned his bone card in the cabin and Pirate Pepi showed him a similar one, according to which the captain was none other than Dr Irene Cunesburry, agent no. 22. For the American intelligence agency. The two organisations practically counted as one in the Anglo-Saxon powers. It was true that she grew up on a ship, but later she managed to get to university as well.

The woman was smoking, and she was looking at the Copper Baron with barely concealed contempt.

"Are you angry, Miss Pepi... Cunesburry?", asked the steersman quietly.

"I merely despise you", she replied sternly. "It should have been your duty to throw me overboard!"

"You are right!", he said with honest remorse. "But forgive me, I could not do it... Look in the mirror and you will find the excuse for my negligent behaviour."

"Who are you anyway?", asked the captain half-jokingly at this provocative tone. "Corvette captain Winter or the rogue Copper Baron?"

"I don't know myself", admitted Milton Winter honestly. "It's often puzzling to me too. Especially, when I attend the admiralty's tiringly monotonous afternoon teas in my uncomfortable dress uniform. Those times I really feel like the Copper Baron disguised as Milton Winter the corvette captain."

It was impossible not to laugh when he presented this so melancholically.

"I would like to know what your opinion is about the André de Rémieux?", asked the woman. "I believe that the Radzeer's arch-rogues did something to the passengers. Perhaps they killed them all."

"I don't think so", said the Copper Baron with an expert's opinion. "They're not that type. They're always into some sort of swindle, but they're basically decent. If the insurance company hired them to guard the passengers, they've perhaps beat one or two or a few valuable items may have disappeared, this is all possible, but they're not the type to just throw away criminal honour... They're all good friends of mine."

"And do you not think perhaps another power could have bought them? Perhaps it's got out that they found traces of manganese ore on the Incognita Archipelago. On the list of passengers the names of some suddenly retired military experts may have appeared... Don't you think so?"

The Copper Baron was sipping his tea thinking.

"Have you heard anything about Dirty Fred, Miss Cunesburry?"

"You mean the captain? As far as I know, he is some respected sea bear..."

"Respected? Hmm... he is many things, but respected?... Anyway. He has a formidable brain. When I was commissioned with the case of the André de Rémieux, I sought out the old man, underneath some barracks, in his private residence. He's not a chatty fellow, but we are on good terms, and he grumbled a word or two about the case. Hold on to your hat, Miss Cunesburry: the solution of the mystery is with Smiley Jimmy! He was on the Radzeer when it accompanied the André de Rémieux and somehow he returned from Cape Blount, and he thinks that we don't know this about him."

"But if you know this.... why did you not have Smiley Jimmy arrested immediately?!"

„It would have been no use, because Smiley Jimmy can be torn to pieces, and he would still not squeal a single word."

„What is your plan?"

„Shall I tell you honestly? I also believe that some swindle took place there beyound Cape Blount, and apart from anything else our first officer is the guarantee for that. My feeling is that the captain passed this commission onto him because he wanted to see what he was going to do, and he is somehow following us..."

„But", said the woman in surprise, „far out in the ocean there has been no sign of a ship for days!"

Milton Winter looked into the eyes of Pirate Pepi:

„After Smiley Jimmy I am the least superstitious person at sea. But I believe it to be more likely that we would see the Green Bloke sitting on the Southern Cross playing the recorder, than the good old Hountler, with Dirty Fred on the bridge, if he does not want us to." And he patted the captain's hand, and she, wondering about the problems at hand, did not appear to notice it, because she tolerated it.

„Tell me please", said the Copper Baron suddenly. „Why did you slap me so hard that my ears were ringing? Why?!"

„Because.. because it offended me", she said bright red, „that for the country... for the Service... you would even make such a sacrifice to... confess your love for me! This was highly improper!"

„Is that so?... Hmm... Thank you for the information." He disappeared for a second, his face in the tea mug, then he faced the woman eye to eye angrily again: „I did not deserve that slap! Know this that my confession was the reflection of my true feelings! Therefore I demand compensation!"

... It was not known how the discussions concluded, but as Dr Irene Cunesburry was a doctor juris, we could assume that she had enough legal background to put right the wrongful mistreatment in a manly manner that befitted Pirate Pepi. This was how it had to be because they stayed together for a long time with the teacups, and the Service was not mentioned afterwards...

Chapter Twelve

As the ship approached Cape Blount, the uneasiness of the crew intensified.

"What do you think the reason could be", one of the sailors asked Smiley Jimmy, "that neither of the disappeared ships sent any radio signals?"

"I think", said Smiley Jimmy, as he did not like the issue to be pursued, "you should take up a position on dry land because of your constant drunkenness, like Halfshoulder Jeff, who sends signals with a flag in quarantine at Ferretown."

And he spat.

"'Cos, for one radio to fall silent", the sailor mulled over the issue without being bothered by this advice, "that happens often. But for two radios not to send a single sound of a signal, that hasn't happened even before the strongest storm."

"You could have absolutely no idea about that because you always drink yourself to the ground before a storm."

And he carried on. This was best. When they sail beyond Cape Blount the atmosphere will change. If only they were beyond it already. There was nothing worse on a ship than whispering.

Especially if it had a point. He sought out Pirate Pepi, who was smiling at him unusually kindly today.

Hmm... It seemed that sooner or later she would notice who was the real man here. Because that he would make a score over this Copper Baron, the guy could make a bet with a funeral association on.

"Listen here", he said with a gentlemanly gesture that he had observed in the royal court, "it would be good to hurry up. How many knots are we doing?"

"We have been sailing at full speed since departure."

"I'm only warning you because it would be good if we were beyond Cape Blount already."

Pirate Pepi smiled at him again and looked him over from head to toe. Smiley Jimmy reached bashfully for his monocle. This woman was so beautiful, as the fresh morning air blew her hair, and lifted her skirt just a tiny bit higher, she was so beautiful that Smiley Jimmy almost forgot this whole Cape Blount business.

"Perhaps you noticed something?", she asked and stepped so close that the frigate captain could very clearly hear as her heart beat heavily.

This woman looked as if she was a different one. It seemed that the Copper Baron could only tell all sorts of rubbish to her, and after all he was only an ordinary sailor, he did not visit royal circles. This sort of thing counted.

"Let them grumble", he replied.

"Do you think there is trouble?", and she put one of her hands on the man's shoulder concernedly.

It was trouble for him already. Smiley Jimmy now earned his nickname not only for his smile, but for his love as well.

"Well…", he stammered bright red, but the woman did not withdraw her hand, how could he talk like that? "There is no trouble at this very moment…"

"Do you think there could be?"

And she put her other hand on Smiley Jimmy's shoulder. She stood quite close to him as if she was instinctively running into the arms of a strong man in her worry. The strong man could not summon a sound into his throat and the blood was hammering in his forehead. About half a minute later he finally spoke.

"You know, these boys are like... how should I begin? So, I finally fixed that pulley that was squeaking."

"I can't thank you enough for being so attentive. To show my gratitude, I'll invite you for tea."

Smiley Jimmy took off his hat and bowed deeply, because this is what he had once seen in Almira when an old lady offered tea to her companion.

"And you mentioned something about the atmosphere amongst the crew."

"Well it would be good to be beyond Cape Blount already. That sort of thing would be useful. But if we are already going at full speed... We can't get further in such a short time."

And he was thinking that one could not get further than an invitation with this woman in such a short time even with the speed of thousand knots.

"As long as I see you, Jimmy, I am not afraid!", said the woman enthusiastically.

"You have no reason to be! One word from you and I will beat up all the scoundrels in the world!"

"I believe there is no need for that."

"But if you do require such a chivalrous service from me, you must know that Smiley Jimmy is ready!"

The woman was left alone because the frigate captain had urgent duties to attend to. Someone stepped over to her from the steersman's room:

"Are you crazy?", whispered the Copper Baron.

"No. But I will extract from this man over a cup of tea what you said could not be extracted from him even if he was cut into quarters."

The Copper Baron, it seemed, was not overly joyous about this idea. Not because he thought that it was basically incorrect, but because he had got engaged with Pirate Pepi two days before.

Two intelligence officers. This would be a rare marriage.

In the evening Smiley Jimmy turned up in his dress uniform, which represented the addition of a single shiny belt to his usual attire. He looked into the steersman's room for a minute.

With a triumphant smile.

"How's the steering?"

"Very good, thank you", said the Copper Baron coldly. "You can stand here from tomorrow. Nobody else can be trusted with it."

"Not that I'm happy about it, but all right. Well, good night!", he said, and with two outstretched palms he pushed his hat to the side, which was already put on sideways cockily.

"Where to with such elegance?"

"To tea", said Smiley Jimmy victoriously. "Pirate Pepi invited me for the evening."

And he waited for the Copper Baron to get slightly dizzy or show his envy or something like that. But the Copper Baron adjusted the steering wheel by two degrees to avoid a large, lazily rolling wave from west, and during this manoeuvre he spit out from behind his cigarette:

"She invited me too. But, it seems she does not like intelligent people because I got nowhere with her."

"You could be right", replied Smiley Jimmy, who misunderstood the reference. "On the other hand I suggest not to get too upset, because there are many pretty women in the docks…"

"Thank you very much for consoling me. But I think I will never forget Pirate Pepi."

"You see, that's how it goes. Women were falling head over heels after you, and this particular one cares not a hoot about you."

"Yes. It's how it is sometimes", replied the Copper Baron more sleepily than sadly. "You are liked by women on ship and on land just the same."

Tea followed.

Smiley Jimmy still remembered the time spent in the royal castle in Almira and he was well aware how to behave at a tea afternoon joined with a gala ceremony.

Let this woman see that an ordinary docks man can be a gentleman in his private life.

"Do you drink tea with rum?", asked Pirate Pepi, who greeted the first officer in an enticing dress.

"Oh, of course! If I could ask for a little tea to go with the rum", said the guest, filling his cup with rum and lifting his little finger elegantly.

"During the first days", said the woman when she poured, "I misjudged you and I only saw later with whom I'm dealing."

"It's usually like that if I may express myself. Women like being flirted with, and this not courtly behaviour is impossible for me. I need to be noticed… I'm sorry!"

He poured his drink all over the woman and their foreheads bashed together. It seemed that the Copper Baron was not paying attention and a big wave hit the ship on the side. Or he was steering a bit more anxiously than otherwise.

"No problem at all, Mr Smiley", Dr Cunesburry, Pirate Pepi hastened to return his elegance. "Things like this happen on ships. And I would like it if we were close intimate friends. It's rare to see such aristocracy in a quarterm... captain."

"This is the results from living in a royal court, I'm sure you know, Miss Pirate, that once I substituted for a real king... I'm sorry..."

Table, glasses, teapot, everything fell over clattering, because a wave hit the ship again on the side.

"It seems that this Copper Baron fell asleep or is drunk!", shouted Pirate Pepi angrily.

"He must have got tired and snoozed off by the wheel", said the guest. In the meantime he tried to put everything back in its place.

"The basis of all friendship with me is honesty", the woman started to cast her net. "You know, between two people it always starts with sharing each other's secrets."

"That is true!", nodded the guest and he blushed deeply when Pirate Pepi sat next to him, and she put her small hands in the first officer's large hand famous from the slaps it hands out.

"Well, you see, it is like that with me in terms of soul and romance, as it is customary in royal circles."

He wanted to drink a little more rum but he did not dare. The devil had got into this Copper Baron today that he forgot how to steer.

"For example I confess to you", lied the woman and put her arms around Smiley Jimmy's neck, "that I am wanted because I took part in the bank robbery in Frisco. There a woman stepped to the cashier first to divert his attention, and that was me. And the armed robbery only started after that."

"Things like that happen…", replied the frigate lieutenant and bravely put his arms around the woman's waist. Pirate Pepi pulled away.

"You have not told me your secret yet. You must have something to hide too."

"I have…", said Smiley Jimmy softly, dazedly. "I hid two crates' of opium in Haiti from the customs officers. If you tell this to anyone, I will face a heavy punishment…"

"Is this your biggest secret? Nothing happened recently…."

The woman underestimated her opponent. Smiley Jimmy stood up, straightened his jacket, he put his handled monocle to his eye, saluted because he really liked doing this.

"Miss Pirate, the pleasure was mine, I was very happy for you to be here, and with your kind permission I am leaving now…"

The Copper Baron was probably not paying attention again, because the first officer tumbled out onto the deck dragging the closed door with him. Pirate Pepi looked after him sadly. Nothing could be found out from this one.

Chapter Thirteen

The great prank started beyond Point Blount. It appeared that some sort of real curse weighed on the ships around here. In the morning Stripy Harry reported to Pirate Pepi that the transmitter was not working. The Copper Baron and the captain, if they were not disciplined to the extreme, would have both stared at Smiley Jimmy. Instead they called Vasich, the world famous mechanic from the engine room. He once did three years just for his mechanic activities.

The mood became a bit gloomy. What sort of a miracle was this? The radios of the two missing ships went silent at the exact place beyond Cape Blount. These men were really not afraid of anything. Not one would have been nervous if they saw a cyclone's swirling, black cloud touching the sea on the horizon. In general, what they could see, they were not afraid of, they knew the risks every time they stepped on board.

But what they could not see but still feel or suspect, made them nervous. It was understandable. On a tiny, puffing, frighteningly dwarfed, man-made creation, always between the vast flat planes of the sky and the sea, a man learnt to lower the flag of his doubt to half-mast against the unknown metaphysical possibilities.

Smiley Jimmy warned his colleagues with a snappy superiority that he had observed from previous strong-minded captains, to keep their calm. Bone Toff scratched his head, spat and replied: 'Absolutely nobody asked you about this, so why're wagging your tongue?'

Red Vasich appeared, he was practically rolling on his bow-legs. On this tiny man only his gorilla jaw and his great curvy nose hanging over his upper lips were of an imposing size. Otherwise he looked more like a jockey than a sailor. Although those who got caught in the melee by this unusually short individual would perhaps remember him as a circus giant in the delirium that followed.

As an echo of Bone Toff's response, Knot Bill said:

"First of all don't wag your tongue because you have the least work here."

"That's right!", added Shirker Hugo. "You and the captain and the Copper Baron sailed this way with the plague ship!"

Smiley Jimmy was indignant, he puffed up his chest menacingly as usual:

"What tales are you telling here? Are you superstitious? In any case, anyone who has a problem with me, just come a bit closer!"

In the meantime Vasich took his coat off to climb to the radio tower, to investigate the cause of the silence. Knot Bill stood right in front of him, and pulled him over by his arm:

"Are you alleging that you were not in that business when Dirty Fred, Smiley Jimmy and the crew of the Radzeer sailed the Green Bloke's sea on that plague ship that they were supposed to burn?"

"Firstly let go of my arm because I'll kick you!", replied the Red. "Secondly that was not the real plague ship, only Dirty Fred conned someone with it and put a fake, warped cover on the Radzeer. This was, if you please, the whole story", he finished calmly, and because Knot Bill was still holding his arm, he hit him on the face so hard that he knocked over Smiley Jimmy as well. Vasich was not a rough-and-tumble man, but he put weight on having his warnings taken seriously. The Copper Baron and Smiley Jimmy had great difficulty holding back Knot Bill, who of course wanted to run Vasich down.

"After all, we must see what happened, there's a great deal at stake", said Stripy Harry, and the mood did not lighten at all following the slap.

The ship was sailing on the Green Bloke's waters, if we wanted to express in a less knowledgeable way, on his home that was made impossible to map because of the constantly changing underwater atoll and coral reefs.

"Where did you hear anyway that the Radzeer sailed this way at all with Fred and I", said the Copper Baron, naming himself as well truthfully, partly to form a proper opposition group with Smiley Jimmy and Vasich, and partly to find out the cause of this suspicious, panicky mood.

The Swedish Ox, an enormous, stocky, relatively calm man, also fell under the effect of the events in this eerie mood. He was the one giving the answer to the steersman.

"Mr Wagner told us the whole case yesterday, and it would have been your duty to warn us!"

"Bravo, strovacheck!", shouted Mr Wagner, who for some mysterious reason had got into the guard tower with door and all. "That's correct, you should have warned us about this, I will tell you… Yes, it was written on the side of the lady-named ship: 'What's with you, you Wagner?'…"

"Now you can see! This moron even forgot the name of the ship that was named after him. We wrote onto the fake cover of the Radzeer with large letters: 'What's up, Mr Wagner?'", shouted the Copper Baron. "Alcohol speaks for this man for many years now, and he has no idea what he's saying…"

"This is not about me! The main thing is that they understand!", shouted Mr Wagner from the guard tower, and he immediately started singing an aria from the opera called Ace of Bells.

The two groups stood opposite each other, half-hostile, when the captain appeared:

"I heard the whole story", she said calmly. "From now on tell everyone that Pirate Pepi is not one who hasn't got the guts of a louse and stayed on board beyond Point Blount. But she allowed the men, that if they wished, we could turn back and they could leave the ship at the next port."

This was a bulls-eye. To have tales told of Swedish Ox, Shirker Hugo, Knot Bill and the others that they were scared to stay on a ship to serve where a woman was not. The grumbling stopped. The Copper Baron secretly squeezed the woman's hand. The rest of them went after their business growling, and Red Vasich, like a monkey, climbed up the radio tower and after some short switching he came down:

"Some sort of giant frigate bird or seagull got tangled up in the radio's cage and destroyed the wiring and the whole shebang with its flapping. The radio is all finished."

"What sort of goddam giant bird could it have been?", murmured the Swedish Ox.

"It was a rare bird, judging from its feathers, that's for sure", replied Vasich, and went about his business. Meaning, that in the dark corridor of the between-decks he waited for Smiley Jimmy, and said quietly: "You Jimmy... The likes of the bird that ruined the radio even my great-grandfather never saw. I brought the feather down..."

"Hmm... What sort of feather did it have!"

"Self-filling!... Upon my honour! Take a look, because you could not see anything like this in a collection: self-filling bird feather. With ink!" And he returned Smiley Jimmy's own fountain pen to him. After a short pause he said: "I'm in this whole smut for a half-share."

"In what smut are you in with half?"

"I don't know that. But with half, you can be sure of that. Cos, if a sailor is so stupid that a wire can pull his pen out of his top pocket when he makes a hash of it, he should take someone else in as well with half."

... What else could he do? Another partner was forced onto him by fate. For his vanity. He had quieted the radio so that the suspense was bigger when a third transmission went quiet beyond Cape Blount in the same way. Incidentally he could also mull over the fact that the Copper Baron and Pirate Pepi appeared to get along really well and whenever they could, they were whispering together in some quiet corner of the deck. It's a dog's business that he was into here.

... The sun rose on a beautiful dry day, which meant the biggest surprise and mystery of the life of each and every participant of this case, including Smiley Jimmy. During the morning three similar gazes scanned the horizon, with the same thought.

Pirate Pepi curiously.

The Copper Baron expectantly.

And Smiley Jimmy with some suspicion.

The captain thought that Dirty Fred could not be anywhere near here because there was not a single line of smoke as far as the eyes could see. The Copper Baron thought that Dirty Fred was very likely near them, somewhere beyond the horizon. Smiley Jimmy was repeating his usual phrase in his head: 'Is this captain stirring it somewhere, or not stirring it?'

But it was useless to look, useless to ponder: the water and the sky did not reply, because they had made a pact with Dirty Fred a long time ago.

The Copper Baron could not move from the steering wheel. There were reefs everywhere, and even early heralds of the approaching polar summer appeared: a few wandering icebergs made it as far as Point Blount.

Far in the distance, at the bottom of the south-east sky, a black strip was visible. That was Incognita Archipelago, where the key to the mystery awaited the passengers of the Blind Dad and through them the entire world. I couldn't say that these grim faces were blinking indifferently at the growing strip on the horizon, but their hardened souls waited stoutly for the events to follow.

At 4.30 pm someone shouted down from the observation tower:

"Upon my word, there is a chimney over there!... A scream of a chimney this is! It grew from some ship seed!"

Through the telescope everyone could see that a chimney was sitting darkly in the island, or on the piece of land belonging to the island, which was green moss all the way to the lush green coast.

"I believe", said the Copper Baron, "that some ship ran aground here and the white vine covered it up. It's not the Radzeer, because the battleship's chimney is narrower."

At 5 pm a surprised voice came from the guard tower:

"I swear on my life that something is swarming around the chimney!"

At 5.10 pm a door fell off the guard tower.

At 5.11 pm a few faded flowers fell after it.

By now the cause of the swarming became clear. A crowd of snakes, microzoa and hideous seaweed creatures covered the piece of land...

"This is a new coral reef", said the Copper Baron. "A small piece of seabed on the surface."

"But however did the ship get into the middle of it?", asked Red Vasich.

Nobody could understand. The person who did understand hurried along to do his rounds in his shiny leather gaiters.

Night was falling. As far as it was possible without the risk of running aground, the Blind Dad navigated close to the piece of land and dropped the anchor. The Copper Baron, Smiley Jimmy and Bone Toff, who was the quartermaster, set off to explore.

They took axes, searchlights and water in a waterproof bag with them in a rowboat.

"First let's see where the Radzeer is", said the Copper Baron when they were rowing towards the shore. They all agreed with his suggestion.

They could see the frame of the André de Rémieux covered in wonderfully green water plants, sunk into the mud, as they rowed around the piece of land with a few strokes alongside the reef. At the end of the reef an exotically lush, flat lava stone island came to view. The Incognita Archipelago. The atoll reef was the continuation of the shoreline under the water which had risen above with such tragically bad timing. It was getting dark. They took out the two searchlights and they looked for the battleship…

They lit every dark spot of the piece of land near them. Suddenly a streak of light shone back from something…

Hurray!

They had found the Radzeer! Her slim chimney was clearly visible… But the battleship herself was covered throughout up to the chimney brim with the lush vegetation of the swamp. She was lying closer to dry land than the André de Rémieux, and the reef here was less covered with seaweed.

"They ran aground in quite a lucky way", said the Copper Baron.

"Hum!...", murmured Smiley Jimmy and turned away to look for something, because he couldn't stand the steersman's gaze.

"I don't even understand", said Bone Toff, the quartermaster, "how could they run aground here, so close to the island."

"Who's interested in your free lecture?!", snapped Smiley Jimmy at him unusually anxiously. "This one wants to know everything better!"

They reached the battleship. First they put on their wellingtons, then they headed to the Radzeer, wading through the seaweed.

When they got closer they discovered that the stony, loose ground contained less white vine and snakes, so much so that the ship's interior was not taken over by the swamp as much as they expected judging from the exterior.

"I just don't understand", wondered Bone Toff, "how come they couldn't get free of this loose ground."

"You don't understand?! What don't you understand?!, snapped Smiley Jimmy. "Perhaps you went to a nautical university that you know something better than others?"

"What are you shouting about?...", protested the quartermaster. "A few people can dig up the reef here under the ship and the tide will drag it off."

"Look at that! The so-smart Bone Toff!... Are you conducting an investigation here?!", Smiley Jimmy snubbed him almost menacingly. "Even a cabin boy on the Radzeer is worth more than you are! You can't dig here because... because the ground is too thin and it fills back up quickly and... And in any case, why are you wagging your infernal tongue over everything?!"

In the meantime a heavy fog fell onto the surroundings.

"Let's not argue now, let's push ahead!", said the Copper Baron.

They climbed up onto the ship.

They did not find a single man on the Radzeer. Here and there screws, parts, crates... Did they perhaps move off the ship?

Smiley Jimmy felt that there was a huge stone in place of his heart. What could have happened to his friends?

Snakes, spiders and water animals swarmed in every corner. The tragedy was largely solved in the captain's quarters.

There had been a fight here!

They sprung back from the doorway frightened as they opened the door.

Everything was broken, smashed, turned over, and on the stretched out map...

Blood!

An enormous, dried, dark spot.

A few days or a week ago a fight to the death took place here.

The Copper Baron disappeared amongst the pile of wreck and rubbish. He crawled around in a squatting position and sorted through the rubbish carefully. Finally he looked at a piece of silk covered with brown blotches, probably blood.

"Were they attacked by natives?", whispered Smiley Jimmy.

"The island is completely deserted. There is no fresh water here", replied the Copper Baron and held the piece of silk to a light.

"Why the hell did these damn tourists come here then", said the frigate lieutenant in a cloudy voice, and he was twiddling his fingers around his neck hesitantly. It was true that in this fog a heavy, greasy heat filled with vapours weighed on them, but Smiley Jimmy had happily given out slaps in much uglier weather conditions before. The situation here was different… The boys were dealt with here badly, that was certain, and this somehow felt heavy on his conscience. Even though the decision was mutual.

"Perhaps some ghost made an appearance this way, if you say that there is no fresh water around here and the island is deserted", murmured Bone Toff.

"Unfortunately, something worse has happened… Do you know what this is?"

Smiley Jimmy looked at the strangely patterned, colourful silk material and expressed his opinion:

"In the royal court small lamps are dressed in things like these, so the king's eyes are not hurt when reading."

"This was torn from an attacker by one of the boys", explained the steersman. "Silk cloak. Which means that Dragon Huang or Wu-Peng got wind of the Robinsons' plan."

The individuals mentioned above were efficient pirates of the islands of the southern sea. They had been smuggling weapons for decades hired by one or another interested party, and because nobody could be certain whether they were on their side or the enemy's, they were almost never made accountable for their crimes.

"What are we going to do now?", asked the quartermaster. "Goddammit that even this radio doesn't work."

Smiley Jimmy swallowed hard and cast a murderous look at Bone Toff. But he said nothing.

"Naturally we will investigate the André de Rémieux as well", said the Copper Baron.

They got back into the rowboat. They had to heave heavily in the enormous globe of that heavy, stagnant, fishy fog. They could not see beyond their noses. They landed on the piece of land around the middle, by guessing the position, from where they could wade over to the steamer. They pulled the rowboat onto land with a grim premonition.

Chapter Fourteen

The end of the wet season was approaching. The unrelenting heat of the sun had been burning the island for two days now, unfortunately also that piece of land which was seabed not long ago. The atoll reef flourished in the sunshine and was pouring out all sorts of smaller and larger monsters in great variety. It took them an enormous effort to heave through the swampy ground covered with puddles, they did not even know whether they were lost, or if any ship had fallen victim to a strange catastrophe around here.

In the meantime the fog started to lift and the torchlight revealed the correct way ahead of them. In wellingtons, with knives and axes, they struggled to move forward in this hell on earth. Snakes, spiders, octopi, and an even more sinister type of white vine spreading all around, was tearing at them, trying to pull them down, and on occasions they sank waist-deep into the swamp of the fresh reef.

When finally they arrived bedraggled, utterly exhausted onto the half-sunk André de Rémieux, they took a rest. Their faces, like raw meat, were bleeding from the bites of the enormous clouds of mosquitos.

The steamer was attracting the inhabitants of an ancient underwater world in her inside protected from the sun. They climbed onto the top deck to do a quick inspection, tripping over reptiles that were rushing out of the way of the torchlight crawling and slithering over each other. There was not much to examine. The steamer, like a happy home, was taken over completely by the parasitic wildlife of the swamp.

They did not find a man dead or alive, just like on the Radzeer.

"How did they want to muck around here for a year without water?", asked Bone Toff.

"They had a distillatory", said the Copper Baron.

"Is that a sort of illness that you can't drink water with?", asked the quartermaster with sympathy.

"A distillatory", explained the Copper Baron annoyed, "is to make fresh water from sea water by way of steaming and cooling."

"I know it", said Smiley Jimmy. "Two years ago I stole a ship, that one also had such a cooling refresher."

"Even if there is no hope, we still must know for certain", said the Copper Baron. "We'll set off to the island."

They had about three more miles in this grotesque underwater hell on land, to get to the island. These well-seasoned men unanimously announced that they would not forget this few-mile trip till the day they died.

In the meantime the fog lifted completely, and the three men finally reached the edge of the new atoll island, a thick woodland. This signalled that before the reef appeared, this was where the shoreline met the sea. The woodland appeared to be an impenetrable jungle on the edge of the island. But a few strikes with the axe, a cut here and there with a machete and the thickness ended. This was just a narrow, round slice of jungle. Heavy, but not deep. Immediately behind it there was normal, thinner vegetation. Only a taste of a wilderness grew here at the edge of the ocean, from the mass of centuries-old rotting and renewing roots, algae, mangrove trees and dead fish.

Water and death, decay and heat: the ancient humus of life could still be found in the tropics, in that rich, boiling state that was the cradle of all life. At the edges of the atoll reefs those interested could still observe the creative tragedy or deadly comedy of nature.

The fog that disappeared as suddenly as it appeared was replaced by a beautiful night. The light of the rising moon spread slowly across the island's volcanic lava stones, the picturesque mass of wattle bushes, saffron, hibiscus and vines. Smiley Jimmy's gaze fell on a couple of unswerving, reedy Palmyra palms.

"I will climb onto one of these to look around just in case", he said to his companions.

None of them believed that any of the unfortunate ones were still alive. They only acted on their conscience. Smiley Jimmy took his shoes off, he grabbed the palm with his left hand, took the axe with his right and climbed… After every crawling move he struck the axe into the damp, smooth trunk. Even the most nimble Malay could not have done it faster. One minute, and he disappeared in the neck-breaking height of green leaves…

The moon lit up the area very well. He looked around slowly and…

He uttered a quiet cry!

The mystery was solved! He saw fires towards the northern part of the island and a few tents. Small figures wearing wide-brimmed hats were cooking something in enormous cauldrons. They were camping behind boulders that were rolled next to each other to create a barricade, opposite a cliff. On the cliff, half way up to the peak, there was a cavern. And in front of the cavern two long pipes. They could only be machine guns!

This was a proper siege.

The besieged ones were most likely the survivors from the shipwreck with the Radzeer's guns!

This camp had to be a band of one of the pirate scoundrels. They were keeping each other at bay. Who knows for how long? He quickly descended, and explained the situation to his companions.

"We will go back to the ship", said the Copper Baron. "We'll bring the men over with guns."

"That's right! We'll get them from the side and if the boys have any brains they will break out at the same time, we can sort these swine out. Are there many of them?"

"Just enough of them, may they burn in hell...", murmured Smiley Jimmy.

They had an easier way back because they headed to the Radzeer that was closer to shore. There was a rowboat on it, that just needed to be cleaned of its inhabitants. This went quickly. The moon went down, with one last chalk-like flash... A dark but clean night fell over the ocean.

They reached their destination in an hour and a half, and they climbed up to the battleship again. It was only a few minutes before the rowboat was ready on the water. The leather bag was not left behind either. Quickly out with the searchlight!

...The rays of light swept the surface of the ocean in a wide semicircle to look for the Blind Dad. The beams were dancing first from right to left, then from left to right...

Then with a restless swirl, right and left and higher up as well, so they could see further away... Well? What was this? The three men sitting in the rowboat were stunned.

In the distant, dark ocean, as far as the light could carry, no ship was visible...

The Blind Dad had disappeared!

Chapter Fifteen

They were talking over each other…

"What could have happened?"

"Perhaps they were also raided and the ship was captured?"

"They left us behind?"

"Perhaps they sailed around the island?"

They felt as if their brains were replaced with a stone. Logic did not have anything to grab onto.

What was this? They could not solve the mystery. This drives one mad. Sense could not even get near them. It was impossible what had just happened. And yet it did happen!

"One of us will go down towards the end of the island, and two of us will go to the western side", said the Copper Baron. "Perhaps they got worried and sailed around the island."

They rowed back to shore.

They landed further up this time, not near the reef. They took a few steps carefully under the cover of the vegetation because they could not know if the pirates suspected that someone else was on the island as well.

The situation was now serious, and taking into account the disappearance of the Blind Dad, it was eerie as well.

"I will go around the island. If the Blind Dad really sailed around and that's why we didn't see her in her place, I will signal the steamer somehow", said Bone Toff and took the searchlight. "You two cut straight across here westwards and wait for me there."

It was better for them to go together, because one going alone could get into trouble easier.

Bone Toff headed due north, and the other two, carrying the leather bag with drinking water and other things, headed towards the opposite shore. Smiley Jimmy was walking with unusually calm steps.

The Copper Baron on the other hand was whistling soundlessly. They made their way carefully, they had to get out of the light of the rising moon which lit the island in a wide semicircle.

"I believe", said the Copper Baron, "it wouldn't hurt to have some sort of axe or knife with us in this godforsaken darkness, in case of any surprises."

They opened the leather bag. The Copper Baron took out an axe and Smiley Jimmy a long, pointy shipwright's tool. They were walking like this alongside each other in the darkness, two enemies, but this did not count now that they were in danger.

Smiley Jimmy was looking at the Copper Baron unusually gloomily. This one first misunderstood it and stepped slightly aside, then asked the question openly:

"Do you want to fight here?"

"This now is not the most appropriate place for things like that... But let's stop for a few minutes."

Smiley Jimmy leant against a tree. It appeared that he was hesitating over something.

"What do you want?", asked the steersman, still in a defensive pose.

"Look... no need to mince words over this, right? It's almost certain that these pirates will do us in. We'll just peek inside the skulls of a few, as it's customary... This is certain because there is no water and the dry season is here. The pirates must have drinking water. And…"

"Spit it out already!"

"So I'll tell you the whole swindle, because if one is done in, it's best to lighten the load of the soul…"

"I don't understand a single word."

"Then you must know that I arrived here with the Radzeer, I just didn't get shipwrecked with them…"

"How can that be?"

"Well… before they ran aground, they took me back to Marquesas so that someone will be able to save them."

"I don't understand!"

… Smiley Jimmy slowly confessed the entire story, as they stood there in the hot, muggy night.

"Hmm!... What a fine swindle!", commented the Copper Baron.

"And you know… now it somehow hurts, it feels like I'm partly the cause of all this…"

"Fool!", said the other, shrugging his shoulders. "Is it you who attacked them or the pirates?"

He lit a cigarette in the meantime and they carried on.

"I will say something as well, Smiley Jimmy, in relation to us not spending much of a holiday here on the Robinsons' island", said the Copper Baron quietly a bit later. "Why should we hate each other when nothing matters anymore?"

"This is very true."

They shook hands. The Copper Baron laughed and Smiley Jimmy put on the smile that earned him his name, and they carried on creeping along the bushes.

They hurried to reach the western shoreline where they were to meet Bone Toff. Suddenly the vegetation rustled behind them…

There was no time to pull a weapon.

"Hands up and don't move…", whispered someone.

And the bleak moonlight seeping through the crown of trees shone on a revolver.

"Smiley Jimmy!...", said the attacker in surprise.

Now they also recognised the stocky man standing in front of them, with his well-recognisable, pig-like face:

"Look, it's Tulip!"

"Quietly!... These scumbags send out raiding parties across the island at night."

"What's the situation up there at the cave?", asked the Copper Baron.

"Their position is a bit sad. I came away a couple of days ago and I can't get back, because these scum tightened their circle around the cliff. But I nabbed three of them, they won't make a sound anymore. With that I got hold of two flasks of water."

"Are you thirsty? We brought water with us."

"I don't want any right now. I just hit a lonely wanderer on the head, that's when I saw your shadows amongst the trees, luckily when I came closer it turned out that you were white. Otherwise it's not my habit to ask questions."

"Let's hurry now so Bone Toff can find us", said Smiley Jimmy.

Far away from the bandits camping around the cliff, they reached a clearing on the west side of the island. Hopefully

Bone Toff, while walking along the shoreline, would not bump into any of these scoundrels.

"The situation is", said Tulip, "that sooner or later, as they've been pondering over it for a couple of days now, they will break out of the cave because they have no water and no food. Dragon Huang's gang is guarding the cliff, may they all drop dead."

A rustling in the bush and Bone Toff appeared in the clearing. There was nothing new that he could say. He saw the Blind Dad was neither on the eastern, nor on the northern or southern shores, and he nearly ran into trouble in the north because Dragon Huang's enormous sailing boat was docked there. The deck was full of water barrels, because they hadn't off-loaded them yet since the rainy season had just ended. He was fortunate that he could hide amongst the bushes to get around the area, because there were a lot of scoundrels patrolling the shore there.

"What can be done here?", pondered the Copper Baron.

"I know their plan", said Tulip, "if you can call a hopeless charging a plan at all. First they will try to get to the bottom of the cliff by splitting into two teams, so that they are protected from all sides from being attacked from behind. Then they will perhaps wait for the night to try and cut their way through... If only one knew which way to cut through on this cursed island."

"Well then, I will tell you the plan of attack!", said the Copper Baron, cutting off any further speculation. "When the boys charge from the cave, we will go in there with pistols, knives, axes and any other weapons we have and we will help a few pass over to the other side in the interest of this case."

"Perhaps we can get close to them after all?...", said Smiley Jimmy.

They were crawling slowly towards the cliff.

"Be careful!...", whispered Tulip. "They have damned sharp ears."

They crawled along carefully for about another twenty minutes, and a few meters from a hedge formed from thick bushes, they stopped at Tulip's signal.

"Are the scoundrels beyond this hedge?", asked the Copper Baron.

"Not one is beyond the hedge. The barricade ends further down. If someone wants to get through the wide hedge, he must first go across the clearing, but even if he reaches the hedge alive, by the time he makes his way through the hedge, a hundred bullets would hit him."

"In that case we could not try to get further than the hedge either."

"Where the hedge meets the cliff, there is a tall, steep granite wall", whispered Tulip. "There's where I descended. But it is unlikely that anyone could get up the smooth cliff..."

They were crouching there puzzled.

"Perhaps it's easier on the other side", suggested Bone Toff.

"It would take us hours to crawl over there. It's better if we wait here until the fighting starts and then we'll throw ourselves in... Because the pirates always charge forward when one moves out. It is more disadvantageous for them on the flat ground..."

"That's good. When it all starts, we will see where we're able to help..."

As if to answer the question, an intermittent sound disturbed the night:

"Ta-ta-ta-ta-ta-ta!"

The machine gun started firing up at the cave. This meant that they were covering the ones tearing down and they were firing into the pirates.

The four men pulled out their revolvers, and in the other hand, where they had one, a knife, an axe, and they charged.

Chapter Sixteen

The group breaking out of the cavern started the battle with the strategy described by Tulip. A battle that seemed hopeless. From the entrance of the cavern two paths led to the grass area. The besieged were running down on these two paths. In front of the cavern one machine gun was firing at the pirates, who were also charging at them in one or two larger groups to finish them off, before they could reach the flat area to the north that was more difficult to control.

But before they could reach them, both groups, covered by the machine gun fire, started building a barricade from the boulders lying around at the ends of the eastern and western slopes.

The moon still lit up the area around the cliff. One of the groups was led by the captain of the Radzeer, the Professor; the other one by Spiky Vanek.

"Where's the spare magazine?", panted Butthead at the machine gun.

They had left it in the cave. That was a big problem! Their machine gun fell silent. As far as they were able to, they fired at the charging pirates with pistols, and Moonlight Charley even with a gun, but it seemed that they could not hold them back with single fire.

Spikey Vanek's group was mainly led by Captain Dorian, one of the tourists. Armed with sufficient spare magazines, they made their makeshift barricade on the other side of the cliff unreachable with the constant flow of bullets. The Professor's group held out bravely, but their situation was desperate. The enemy had probably reached the barricade by now.

They had no dead yet, but Busy Weasel received a bullet in his left arm, whilst he was flourishing two revolvers, and between his teeth, like a Sioux, he was holding a kitchen knife, to be ready for all eventualities.

"Let's pull back!", shouted Butthead.

"We can't! If we're defeated up there, they could attack Spikey Vanek from behind."

The enemy reached near the barricade, with great leaps, from time to time throwing themselves left and right behind some form of cover. There was a wild exchange of fire. A stray bullet scalloped Fat Peter's earlobe. Many pirates lay on their bellies all around, and would never get up again to continue the fight. But a small group was crawling and skipping fast towards the barricade. The last few steps were a mad run, without any consideration.

The first one that jumped onto the pile of stones was hit by the Professor on the head with the machine gun, which he had reclassified as a battle axe with a sudden decision, so hard that he fell back with his skull completely squashed. But the next moment another two, then three ran up the barricade, these also fell at the counterattack by the Professor and Butthead, but another four or five came to replace them, and their situation seemed hopeless. Two of them were already fighting inside the stone pile, about ten of them reached the cliff, where only a few meters of path separated them from the barricade, and a two-meter giant broke away, jumping up on the stone pile, he wagged his ancient rusty blade above his head, ready to strike…

…At that moment, from somewhere in the darkness, with precision, an axe arrived in a hurry and spattered his skull.

The charging bandits were scattered by twenty or thirty volley fires from the direction of the hedge from where they did not expect an attack and from where they were vulnerable.

The remaining few attackers ran away as quickly as they could to find cover. And the rescuers emerged from the hedge…

Behind the barricade they quickly took count of the result of the attack. Butthead was bleeding from a thorough sword cut that run across his face from his right eyebrow through the base of his nose to his left jawbone, the Professor's forehead was scraped by a bullet, the stoker of the tourist steamer was finished by a knife. The other seriously wounded was the first officer of the André de Rémieux. Two sailors, as far as it was possible in the situation, tried to bandage the officer's serious shot to the lung.

The Professor was only pressing his handkerchief onto this forehead, and he was looking at the death-faced, skeleton-like Moonlight Charley in amazement:

"Did you throw that axe?"

"Are you blind? It was thrown from behind the barricade, and I swear on my life that someone fired at the scoundrels from the bushes. Without that all of us would have bitten the dust."

"Who the devil could have been?"

In the meantime the four-member rescue group climbed the path to the barricade.

"Don't shoot!...", said someone quietly from behind the rock pile.

Ten guns ready to shoot turned towards the voice.

"Hurray!", said the Professor. "It's the Copper Baron! How many of you?"

"The whole inventory is here", said Smiley Jimmy, while the four of them emerged and quickly jumped behind the rocks.

The cliff was covered in dust straight away from the late bullets that greeted the new arrivals.

"We had a good look around!", panted Tulip.

"What's on the other side?", asked Fat Petters in his painful, high-pitched, croaky voice.

"They could not even get close to them, Spikey Vanek was cutting them down with the machine gun", replied the Copper Baron.

"It's lucky that we broke through the hedge on your side, otherwise none of you would be alive by now."

"We left the spare magazines back there, otherwise they couldn't have even gotten close to us", said Butthead sadly, and he tore a bandage from his shirt as the cut was bleeding heavily at the base of his nose. "A few of us got it bad."

"The poor stoker is done."

"I think the first officer won't make it till morning either", said Moonlight Charley, who started cleaning his weapon.

They all wanted to hear from Smiley Jimmy what sort of expedition arrived to their rescue, but the Copper Baron and Bone Toff, as well as the few passengers there from the André de Rémieux could not hear about the case. So they tried to relay their curiosity by eye contact.

Their mood turned overcast when after a few of these meaningful glances Smiley Jimmy finally started talking. They learnt that the expedition sent to find them had disappeared with ship and all. And there was no way to solve that mystery.

Unfortunately, everything there was as they thought. The defenders had not a single drop of water left. The last flask was left in the cave, where an old professor, a little black boy and two women stayed behind. They were in a very distressed state.

Part of the mystery was solved for the three-member 'rescue party', as the Professor started telling them the events up till now.

"The thing is that these are not really tourists… They were looking for some miracle stone. An ore called manganese. And the problem was that they were secretive. It started with us also running aground, and somehow or another, luckily, at a flatter part, where it was a bit more shady." He cast a quick look at Smiley Jimmy. "We decided, naturally, to go over to the other shipwreck."

"Could you not dig out that small battleship in the loose ground, enough for the tide to take it down?", interrupted Bone Toff, because he could not understand how that was possible. "It's barely tipping on the edge."

A few of them looked at him. Not exactly at the same time. Not exactly in a friendly way.

"How lucky we are", said the Busy Weasel venomously, "that you haven't forgotten to bring along a sailing expert! Because that's what we missed the most."

"In any case", said the Professor to Bone Toff, "why are you wagging your tongue at everything? Are you someone of importance as well?"

"All right, all right, just carry on!", said the Copper Baron.

In the meantime morning came, and the sun arrived with hot rays to torture the already exhausted people.

"So", explained the Professor, and took off his jacket, "our ship (what good luck!) ran aground at a quite good place. Naturally we visited the tourists immediately to check if they needed help. Then time went by. We waited for a rescue. These fellows, amongst them an old scientist and others, are not much use in places like this. They searched the inside of the island with pickaxes, and on the ship they had a water-making whatsit…"

"Distillatory", Bone Toff applied the technical term he heard earlier. "It creates drinking water from sea water by destitution…"

It was his doom to talk again. Moonlight Charley, who's been cleaning his weapon, cast a spiteful glance at him:

"I can't stand this constant lipping of yours. Since when are you an expert? You're observing everything like a police inspector."

"And there's not much of a future for a police inspector on a lonely island if he meets us!", added Busy Weasel grumbling. Bone Toff did not understand why his friends hated him all of a sudden, so he started explaining:

"I'm just saying that the battleship was lying in the sand…"

"Listen here!", said the deathly-faced, two-meter tall Moonlight Charley, and raised his rifle butt at him. "How the battleship is lying in the sand, perhaps you know better than us. But how you will lie in the sand if you don't stop flapping your lips and I climb onto you with the rifle butt, that's not in question."

At this Bone Toff took out his knife, the Copper Baron hit aside the rifle butt that Moonlight Charley raised to hit him, and Smiley Jimmy also intervened with all the anxiousness of his heart in the interest of peace and caught Bone Toff in the mouth so that he tottered into the nearby bushes, and with this tempers chilled, because the entire crew of the Radzeer felt this punch building in their fists.

It was said that Bone Toff was pondering on this even to this day, he could not understand why he received that incredible slap just for meaning well, but nobody explained it to him because the Radzeer's mission was buried by time along with the reef, like so many other events from the past of these grim men.

"Now, carry on!", said the Copper Baron, after he cast a look towards the bandits' camp. It was morning and the sun was shining hotly. They did not move from behind their barricades. Why should they fight? The dry weather would yield the fruit of the lack of water without them risking anything: the castaways.

"It was like this", continued the Professor, "that many of the tourists caught fever, because even though they built a ramp the swamp spread over it from one day to the next, and they had to go to the island every day across this mud puddle and back. So most of them moved into this cave, we took the distillatory over to our ship because this (how lucky is that) ran aground on a drier part closer to shore, and this is where the lads took the distilled", and he poked towards Bone Toff disdainfully, "therefore not destitute drinking water. But by then so many of them were ill that they had to resort to put us to work as well."

"What sort of work?", asked Smiley Jimmy.

"Well this one must be kept like a military secret. It is not the first time that the Secret Service made use of us. Here on this island a painter realised that a certain manganese ore was found. As I mentioned before, that's some sort of technological raw material thing like an oil source, or perhaps guano. Important for weapons. And these tourists are not tourists, but Secretive Servants, and so many of them came down with fever that they had no option but to employ us, and they explained what sort of stone could have manganese ore. So we also dug with mattocks and spades, as some of us got well trained on these in the good old days in Sumbava, because this sort of work is called useful employment in a penal trade colony."

"And how many people say", murmured Busy Weasel mockingly, "that a criminal background is detrimental in public service. We wouldn't have been much use without the routine of Sumbava."

"Shut up!", the Copper Baron warned his companion, "so many of you are talking that one cannot understand a thing. So you helped them search for manganese ore?"

"We were digging here and searching. Then the ambush happened! There was nobody on the André de Rémieux by then, but it is a good old habit of ours to have guards in the tower at all times. Therefore the arrival of Dragon Huang's scoundrels did not hit us entirely unexpectedly. The first attack, when they thought that they would have an easy job with surprise on their side, we batted back so that it would take until the day they die for many of these scum to forget if this date was not already a day in the past. So we retreated for the night. But we knew well that when morning arrived, they would surround us and try to attack us more wisely from two sides. Furthermore there were a great many of them, there was nothing else to do: so during the night we dismantled the machine guns and took from the ship whatever we could. So slowly, carefully, we also retreated here to the cave from the Radzeer because she (how lucky is that) was stranded on the reef advantageously. At least they could not attack us from the back on the cliff. We had no problem with the water either initially because it rained all day. But it seems that the dry season has arrived."

The Professor ran out of breath. Sultry heat rose slowly. Moonlight Charley, who was cleaning and oiling his weapon with blinding precision as usual, finished the story.

"Of course the dogs got a sniff of what happened, and as you can see, surrounded us and the deadly competition began. Would a rescue expedition be here first, or would the dry season arrive and fry us out of the cave?"

The Copper Baron slapped his hand onto his forehead:

"Good God! We had some…"

"What?"

"The flasks!…"

Bone Toff and Smiley Jimmy shouted out at the same time.

Because they also brought a few flasks of water from the ship in the leather bag, but they lost it on the way. And they were already covered in sweat, their throats and tongues were dry as torchwood. They sat even more disheartened amongst the rocks, on the smooth, burning lava cliff.

"We can't do anything now!", said Moonlight Charley, and his voice rattled dryly in his throat. "Perhaps one of us can sneak out in the evening to get water…"

He ran out of breath.

The air was burning with a killer heat. Dorian, a captain, who was suddenly 'retired', so he could take part in the search for manganese ore, returned. He was up at the cave, where they left the helpless with the last of the water.

"Professor Hughes", he said sadly, "will not make it till evening if we can't get water. There is not a drop of it left up there either."

"We'll pull straws", suggested the Copper Baron. "One of us will sneak out to find the lost leather bag. We left it at the clearing on the western shore where we met Tulip."

This suggestion was more or less in line with their ethical thinking. Those who made an error in something must put it right. A coin was flipped, a thud… The Copper Baron won against Smiley Jimmy!… The quartermaster flipped the coin again, and (just the fate of the frigate captain) he lost again. The croaky Petters turned menacingly towards Bone Toff:

"This one is a university professor in everything! Until someone cuts his knowledge with a knife…"

In the meantime Smiley Jimmy disappeared. He skilfully slid down to the bottom of the barricade. It was difficult to get through the semicircle of the blockade. Although the semicircle did not close off near the cliff, on both sides thick bushes made it impossible for anyone to slip through unnoticed. If there was a noise in the bushes, it would be covered in volley fire by the robbers. There was not much to think about here. It was a game of chance. Fortune favours the brave.

Or misfortune. No matter. At the bottom of the cliff that giant pirate's body still lay. He crawled over carefully. This giant body had to be dragged to the nearest boulder inch by inch in a way that the guards did not notice anything. The vegetation after the rainy season was lush, and the stunt was somehow successful. Smiley Jimmy's efforts were noticed above and at the Copper Baron's suggestion they put the enemy's barricade under heavy fire.

It worked with warships. Fake fog from gunpowder. In the sweltering, breezeless heat the smoke from the guns spread slowly. Smiley Jimmy pulled on a pair of slacks and a blood-splattered silk cloak, a wide-brimmed straw hat was just lying there as well. Now he openly jumped towards the robber's barricade, hiding behind whatever cover he could find. His face was covered completely by the wide rim of the hat. The bandits didn't fire at him because they thought that one of their wounded mates came to and wanted to get back. There was fire immediately from the opposite barricade, but they took care that they aimed elsewhere…

…Now as if he wanted to escape the heavy shower of bullets, he turned sideways, jumped behind the bushes, and the pirates were even cheering him on. Then… just a second, wading through shrubs and thorns, he escaped from the blockade. He quickly rushed towards the bank, and hurried to reach the camp site along the shore. There was the group of Palmyras… From behind, from the direction of the Radzeer, they chose the spying spot by this group of trees. He estimated the direction of the campsite and threw himself into the thicket. He was groping around leaning down. He had to succeed in the pitch dark of the adjoining tree crowns. After a few minutes, by some strange luck, he found the leather bag. He quickly kneeled back up and…

He was hit on the head behind with a door so hard that he collapsed half stunned and he could still hear the attacker shouting:

"What a sweet strovacheck! He arrived as per schedule, I'd say… Oops, my little pigeon, don't jump about!... You can get as many on your head as you want, I'm very generous about that…"

And before Smiley Jimmy could manage to get up, Mr Wagner, justifying his aforementioned generosity, hit him on the head about twice more so that he fell to the ground unconscious…

Chapter Seventeen

The second group on the other side of the cliff was also dying of thirst behind the machine gun stand and barricade. Captain Dorian, who, despite the lack of water and heat, did not spare himself from exercise, kept going from place to place to keep people's spirits up, which was a fruitless effort in this hopeless situation.

"It will be evening within minutes", he said to Spiky Vanek, who was still on his feet, it's true that was only by leaning against the barricade, but he was smiling still with his chapped, swollen mouth.

"It will be evening", replied the sailor. "There will be sunrise tomorrow, but there will no sunset for us anymore."

"Your friends hold up well, it's only the 'civilians' that are the problem. The engineer is in the worst state... What the devil is this?!"

The marauders eyes and mouth fell wide open. Such a miracle was not seen in the world before! From the bushes to the west a madman appeared unexpectedly!

He was wearing slacks that were open up to his armpits, above it he wore a yellow silk cloak, on the other hand he was wearing a pair of altogether ragged, elephant-feet-sized black shoes, a black top hat; and what was frightening like some hallucination that he carried a door like a briefcase, holding it lightly to his right. If his appearance was not so surprising, it was possible that a volley fire would have finished him immediately, but this way it was fired late. He sped up his large, calm steps, which were high at the same time so he would avoid tripping over his flappy, cumbersome shoe soles, and walked to the barricade, but he let out a loud cry beforehand and raised his hat:

"The Spiky strovacheck! Good day!... It is always an honour to meet a great rascal.... Would you look at that! Good God! These here are firing real bullets!" And he jumped behind the barricade panting. "It's a death-trap to stroll around here..."

Spikey Vanek explained the blue-bearded, frightening arrival in a struggling, heavy voice:

"This is a loopy world-travelling tramp... Alcohol could finish him off any second for about twenty years now...", and after a short panting he turned to Mr Wagner: "How the hell did you get here?"

"You see, you're right about that! I was charged by my old great Cap'n, the Pirate Pepilia, the queen of the sailing captains, she said: 'Look, you Wagner, my outstanding chum, would you please sit in a rowboat, row, my buddy, to the island, there are three men there, all great rascals, a jolly good sort, the Smiley Fred and the Bony Copper Baron and the Toff Oliver! Tell them, pal, that I will go to an island to bring water!... And they should not worry because I'm fine.' So I brought this message!... She said all sorts of other things as well but it's not worth remembering. The main thing is that you should not worry here because she is fine, just went to get some water, but it's possible that this will pass because she's got a strong constitution..."

"Water!...", rattled an unconscientious sailor.

"Here you are! This one sent so much with me that it makes no sense..."

A miracle.

Mr Wagner opened his cloak and across and all over him, he was wearing about eight giant flasks!

Chapter Eighteen

The worn out men all moaned at the same time instead of crying out. Dorian ran with a few flasks first to the cave, then to the other barricade...

Water! Water!

The last wide rays of the angry-red sun burnt the island, and life and strength returned to the bodies halfway to their graves...

Spiky Vanek wiped his mouth and held the flask to Mr Wagner:

"Drink, old friend! You really do deserve water."

The old, wrinkled, warty face looked at Spiky with a deep sadness:

"Did I hurt anybody?", he said mournfully. "Why do you want to torture me?... Take that water strovacheck to the pirates because I swear on my door I don't know you anymore."

And he took out his two-litre rum bottle from his pocket and took a good draught. To get anything else out of Mr Wagner in relation to Pirate Pepi's message was a fruitless effort. But what else could she have said? It was right to go and get water, but by the time she returned from the nearest island, there would be no living soul amongst them.

Night fell. The blue-beard was tottering left and right guffawing. He was greeted with subdued enthusiasm in the other camp:

"Do you know if the Blind Dad could bring some help somehow?", asked the Copper Baron.

"Pardon?... They were probably going to a police station!... That woman talks so much that one cannot understand half of it."

There was no point to hope. The woman wanted to bring water, and she sent Mr Wagner with the message because he was the only one dispensable, and the person actually to be dispensed on board. It was impossible to hope. The nearest place was the far-away Marquesas Islands, but these few flasks would not last at all. They would not even get half way and there would be no living person left.

... The next day, rationing their water almost to the drops, they waited idly in their hopeless situation, dispirited, agonising. They were waiting for Smiley Jimmy. Because who could have suspected that Mr Wagner whacked him on the head with his door a few times? And if Mr Wagner was not asleep in the parched morning, pulling his door over him? If he talked about his adventure by chance, or say Smiley Jimmy returned with some water? Would it matter? Their fate was sealed by the heat and their situation.

"We've been foolish!", muttered the Professor.

"But at least we're not doing any other foolishness in life. Or anything else", mumbled Moonlight Charley and peeked inside the rifle barrel to check if the wiry, long brush had oiled the bullet tube properly. They sat in silence because there was nothing else to talk about...

Down there, in a semicircle, behind the barricades the armed marauders were ready. Further away around the leader's tent some commotion appeared to begin. Or did they just gather around to chat?

The first officer of the André de Rémieux was spent. They buried him at the bottom of the cliff, as honourably as they could manage. It was doubtful if there would be anyone to bury them.

One eventless, dispirited hour followed another….

All of a sudden Moonlight Charley shouted in a frightened, sharp voice that they never heard from him before:

"Look over there!"

They all looked in the direction of this outstretched arm. Towards the slopes leading to the cliff. And they remained there with wide open eyes, drooping mouths, stupidly, incapable of a single sound in their astonishment, stunned, as if they all turned insane and they all saw the same vision.

A lonely man approached indifferently from towards the enemy camp.

This lonely man was Dirty Fred! The captain!

… He was walking with his coat draped over his lower arm, his hands in his pocket, his upper body swaying, unconcerned, looking at the pebbles falling apart around his feet, as if he was walking towards the nearest pub in some alleyway in Frisco. When he reached the barricade, he looked at the company with some distaste, nodded towards them with his chin and said:

"You can pack now, you're going home."

Chapter Nineteen

What happened to the Blind Dad?

The immensely calm sky and sea could not have swallowed her, for sure.

The most likely theory was that the Green Bloke intervened (who occasionally took the steamers he liked onto the edge of his long black cloak reaching to the bottom of the horizon), but that later also proved incorrect. Although Shirker Hugo heard him play the flute, and before the moon rose above the edge of the sea, for a few seconds he also saw a skull grinning benignly with a white glow, and it had to be like that because he was extremely drunk and in this condition he could see clearer than otherwise. But according to Shirker Hugo the Green Bloke merely inspected the ship, but it seemed that he did not like the steamer because he sunk back below the edge of the sea instead of taking her down.

The Blind Dad's mysterious disappearance on that night happened like this.

When the rowboat of the three men was covered by the evening dusk, the usual drawling life of an anchored ship began with foreseeable uneventfulness. Shirker Hugo was mending his sweater, Red Vasich finally dismantled the engine part smoking in cart-grease around the bearings, where some rattling noise that did not belong there had annoyed him since Tahiti. The Stripy was sitting in an airing window with his trousers folded up to his knees and was washing his legs. Occasionally a seagull, as it was circling around low, fell sideways on its wings, like some tiny version of the latest model of dive-bomber, and swooped down onto the food waste streaming out of the kitchen pipe.

Pirate Pepi remained standing in the same place and the same way since she saw the three men disappear in their rowboat. She was staring into the darkness, waiting for their return. She had a heavy feeling writhing between her heart and her throat. She felt danger in every nerve of her body. And waited for the return of the melodic voice of the Copper Baron, that slow, deep ringing voice which frequently ended in a quiet laughter.

But it was no use waiting there, leaning against the railings.

Only the water splashed occasionally as a wriggling flying fish threw itself upwards and fell back again. In the meantime deep fog fell over the ocean. Who knew how long she stood there rooted to the place? Hours went by. Later she suffered from a headache from the thick fog, opened the door to her cabin and…

And she was unable to move in her surprise! She stood rooted to the doorstep in dismay, she thought she was dreaming…

An astonishingly dubious looking, bearded old man sat at her table, drinking her rum.

"Have you heard of me?", asked the goateed man without any introduction. The woman knew at that moment who this was.

"Dirty Fred!"

"The captain", he completed it grumbling. "We must act quickly, therefore I inform you that I am your superior, Miss Cunesburry…"

Not a word was true from this. He had searched through the woman's belongings during his short stay and he wanted to avoid a lengthy persuasion, because this type usually made a lot of objections.

"You know my name…"

"I just told you that I am your superior at the Service, rear admiral Anderson sent me. There's not a minute to waste."

"How did you get here?"

"The Hountler approached this old tin can with not much clamour and a darkened deck. Shall I tell you now that I rowed over, avoiding making a noise, climbed up on the anchor chain... I don't like a lot of talk. Do you have more rum?"

"No... But here's some whisky. So", she started anxiously, "three men rowed to shore."

"I know about that. Don't worry. Once I'm here none of the rascals can get into any trouble. But you have an important part to play in this case. You must return to the Marquesas at full steam and bring back as much fresh water as the ship can carry. If you find another vessel, put it on tow and water, water, water, as much as you can, and as quickly as you can, otherwise even I may not be able to help. There's about ten days' worth for the whole company, perhaps we can halve that somehow."

"And the ones at shore right now, the Copper Baron and..."

Dirty Fred took out his palm-sized, ancient pocket watch from his back pocket:

"Let's synchronise watches. I don't care for chit-chat. If you don't set sail within ten minutes, I will hold you responsible for everything that happens from now on. My watch shows 50 minutes past 11. Good night!"

With this he turned around and left Pirate Pepi, with just a poke at his cap, which a well-meaning observer could count as greeting.

By the time the woman rushed out after him, she could not see him anywhere. He disappeared the same way as he came: unnoticed, suddenly, like some vision...

12 o'clock.

... Dirty Fred was chewing on the dog-end of a fag impatiently on the bridge of the Hountler. Not many would have been able to see that dark contour in the even darkness of the night that the captain's gaze watched... Then this hairline, distant contour, the Blind Dad, shook, separated, and melted into the darkness slowly... The hawk-fingered, hard, old hand slid from the beard, reached to the speaking tube and muttered into it:

"Full steam!... Half right!... Ahead!"

And the deadly game began.

Chapter Twenty

Dragon Huang was sipping his tea nervously in his tent. He had been stranded here for weeks now, he'd lost more men on this venture than if he'd attacked a well populated island, and he suspected already that before he finished his task, more of his men would bite the dust. The devil take those scoundrels with the battleship! If those sea marauders were not there, he would have concluded the business a long time ago and he would be home. He announced this to the European guest in his tent, a thin, bony, tall individual.

"I must get much more money. You did not say that this cursed Radzeer would also play into this case."

"I did not know either", muttered the European. "Inconceivable misfortune, that chaps like that were also involved in the case."

"My best men fell."

"As compensation, you will receive twice as much as I promised when the fighting is finished!"

Now Juan-Fen, the pirate's first man rushed into the tent anxiously.

"Great Huan! A rowboat came to shore from a steamer... that disgusting white wizard, who we call the Dragons' Unclean Father."

"Dirty Fred!", said the pirate leader dumbstruck. "Bring him here."

Dirty Fred stepped into the tent as if he entered the café at the Royal Park in Southampton for a coffee. He murmured something and he touched his cap here as well, so it could be taken as a greeting by anyone who wanted to.

"What do you want, Dragons' Unclean Father?... I am warning you that I will have you shot at the first suspicious move."

"I don't recommend it", he said with good intent. Then he sat down and poured tea for himself. "In any case I thought that I am your friend, Dragon Huang. I drank to that with you, in your house."

"That's true... But you always think something else than you say."

"Well, now I will prove it that you are mistaken", replied the old man, nodded, drank the tea and said: "Because we are friends, I promise you that if you don't make a fuss and all your men put their guns down, then: so be it! I will let you run, although I was promised a lot of money for you in Java."

Dragon Huang jumped up, he unsheathed his old palm_leaf-shaped blade.

"Do you want me to cut you in two?"

"I would like to avoid that", he replied and poured tea again. "You know me well, and I know you well. You know that if I say something like that, I have good reason for it."

"And I wouldn't like to kill you because you are a cursed wizard and your blood will bring bad luck to my sword."

"That's the least that will happen to you after my death."

"Damn it!", interrupted the European, who considered this long conversation stupid. "Tell me why you ordered Dragon Huang, this dreadnought leader to surrender."

"Who are you?", asked Dirty Fred and inspected the European.

"This gentleman is my friend and my guest…"

"And he's the one who offered you money for the ambush… Just stay sitting there calmly, because by the time you reach for your revolver, you're a dead man…"

Both Dragon Huang and the European stood there perplexed, and as usual, Dirty Fred dominated the situation without any weapon or force.

"Tell me, why did you come and why did you threaten me, even though I am your friend?", asked the pirate leader.

"I picked up some radio signals with some of my men on a whaling ship. You can imagine that I did not come here to mount an attack on you with the Hountler. But the fifteen thousand tonne warship Southampton is heading here full steam to deal with you and your men."

"That's not true!", said the European. "A mere bluff!"

"You keep your mouth shut when respectable dragons talk", said Dirty Fred.

Dragon Huang did not particularly like the European, as it became clear from the preceding events. This matter however concerned him first of all:

"You are just saying this to mislead me", he said to Dirty Fred, "because you want to help my enemy."

"If you don't believe me, that's fine. I warned you. There are English aristocrats amongst the passengers of the André de Rémieux."

"By the time help arrives, we'll finish them!", shouted the pirate leader. "In any case you are famous for never telling the truth, and sometimes you befuddle people with this and defeat them…"

"The whole thing is a bluff in my opinion as well", said the European. "The warship Southampton would not be used for such a purpose."

"All the same to me. I warned you, Dragon Huang, because you are my friend, and I drank to that in your house", Dirty Fred covered his retreat. "That is known on every sea and that's why I came here. Just for friendship."

"I will let you go free if you return to your ship immediately and leave the island. Because you are the type that if you think up something you can thwart all my speculations."

Dirty Fred was led back to shore under heavy guard, where he sat back in his rowboat. It was the Hountler's boat. He untied it from the root where he tied it up when he arrived and rowed back to the whaling ship anchored not far away. He was in a bit of a bad mood because his bluff did not work. Still, he should save these men somehow…

A rope ladder was lowered from the ship and the old man started to climb.

Chapter Twenty One

The ship pulled far away from the island. During this time the sortie of the besieged took place, who considered their situation hopeless, down at both ends of the bottom of the cliff. Dirty Fred was partly holding talks with his men, and partly thinking next to his bottle of rum. He thought that he could simply scare the pirates, but this was unsuccessful.

When something finally started to take shape in his brain…

Crack! Engine troubles. The Hountler came to a halt. Treacherous seaweed twisted and twirled around the propeller until they completely covered it and it stopped working. And in the machine working at full speed something cracked, broke, snapped…

The captain was swearing colourfully!

Many men's torturous death would follow if the engine fault could not be repaired quickly. A sailor, tied onto a rope, made rapid dives down to the propeller to cut the white vines, and he managed successfully not to attract the attention of the sharks swarming nearby. It was tedious work. At dawn another sailor took his place. Repair works continued in the engine room. It was difficult. They could not try the result of their efforts while the propeller was motionless, and the engine was idle. Gunfire drifted towards them from the island… and the hours passed by, time went, until finally the Hountler headed towards the northern corner of the island with a great delay.

They sailed on until they spotted Dragon Huang's enormous sailing boat, where rows of water barrels stood on deck. They were put there during the past stormy days, according to old sailing customs, to collect the rainwater and thus replenish the water supply with the plentiful tropical rain. They merely lifted the lid off the barrel when it started raining and put it back on when the sun came out.

The Hountler slowly returned and set off along the shoreline, almost bored, seemingly aimless, parallel with the enormous sailing boat. Although Dragon Huang forbade this, but what harm could a ship do here. Nobody gave a toss. A few barefoot men with no weapons on a small steamer, she didn't even have a cannon… what could she do?

But they did not know that Snout Eugene was there. The famous Snout Eugene!

An outstanding harpoonist!

And there was the hydraulic harpoon machine. Strangely three of them stood next to each other. This was how they mounted them in a hurry. There were quite a few knotted lengths of rope wound up for the harpoon, so if they hit a whale, it would unravel after it. Foolish men, they had prepared the spare guns already. At least this is what those could have thought who were not adept at it. Who took the trouble to observe that they also attached three pointed whaling grenades to the harpoons? And anyway: who was fool enough to pay attention in this heat?

The Hountler slowly reached in line with the sailing boat. The captain stood in his place and shouted into the speaking tube indifferently:

"Full steam! Forward!"

At the same time: Baaang!

A pop, and the whistling of the ropes whizzing through the air… The first harpoon found its way amongst the barrels…

Zumm! Splash!… The grenade exploded!

Boom… Brrr… Boom!!

An enormous explosion shook the island.

Because, as the steamer got to the opposite side of the sailing boat, quickly one after the other three harpoons whistled into the mass of water barrels laid out on the schooner's deck. And the explosion that followed destroyed the water reserves so that there was not a day's worth of water left amongst the splintered planks.

Then the main mast slowly, as if an epilogue to the main event, fell over full length, tearing all the main sails with it. And the Hountler sped along in a wide circle to quickly get out of firing range.

Dragon Huang listened to the report numbly. Then it was announced that someone came all the way to shore from the Hountler. Dirty Fred arrived.

Alone!

"I came to you to talk, Dragon Huang", he said calmly.

"I will now fry you on the campfire!"

"You can eat me alive if you like", said the old man indifferently. "But what will you drink after me?"

"Wretch!"

"So as I said, Dragon Huang", he continued and convivially poured tea for himself. He paid no attention to the European. "As you are my friend, I will let you run away. I have a foolish heart, what can I do? But you must put down weapons within the hour. My sailors are all cowards, so you will only get water from the Hountler if I return and I reassure the men not to worry. You will then be able to take a half-ration of water for each man on a rowboat, and when the supply arrives from the Marquesas, you can load enough for the way home. In the meantime the Radzeer's crew will stand guard over you and your men. You are a wise man, why would you argue?... So gather the guns in the middle of the clearing by the time I return. I will now go to have a word with those, by the cliff."

This was a clear case. Dragon Huang would not have been a seasoned leader if he spent his time with useless rage and stamping. Especially in a heat like this, with so many men. Everyone was already thirsty, now that they knew there was no water.

... Before the hour was up all the weapons were piled up and the besieged became victorious. They deployed in a semicircle around the pirates, ready to shoot.

An unremarkable incident also happened. Somewhere, in an undeterminable position, a gun went off, and a bullet found the European originator's head. Nobody felt sorry for him. The pirates, just like the shipwrecked, could blame him for all their troubles.

... Dirty Fred stood by his word. What could he do? He had a foolish heart.... When the Blind Dad arrived, he supplied Dragon Huang, his old pal, with sufficient water and let him run.

The reunion of Pirate Pepi and the Copper Baron was the best reward for their brave efforts for both of them.

But the greatest gratification and reverence was due to the Captain.

The entire crew of the Radzeer gathered and decided that before they sat sail home, because (how lucky is that!), they had successfully freed the battleship from the reef: they would seek out the Captain and solemnly recompense him for catching him stealing back in the old days.

But by the time they went down to the beach at dawn, the Hountler had already pulled up the anchor and not even her smoke was visible on the horizon.

Chapter Twenty Two

His Majesty
Samtonio high prince sir (and kyng)
Almira Castle
Blistful Island

Dear Mr Kyng and honourable relatives!

I got back in Tahiti the manifestation of your graceful royal loyalty. There was a grate prank since then! I don't know if I mentioned before that there is tis captain named after him who always messes. You will not believe this! He was in it yetagain! And from the behind! Because he has got so crooked a brain (inhis head) that no proppeler can turn as much in number.

This one simpely back in Frisco when we spoke knew why I was there and what for (for as I mentioned, but he did not know this one). And tis one followed us with that carcass boat becase I am very angry at him now becase there were so many of us that there was barely money for each, even though this Copper Baron named steersman married the captain and as wedding present he gave us his share and we even inherited the reward because he married, the poor man.

I arrived safely onto the Rotbison Kruso island, with the Copper Barron and Bone Toff (I don't know if your majesty chummed up with him, this is our kind of bloke, only he keeps barking about machinary all the time and that's not tolerated on the Radzeer), so by the time we got back to the

Archipelago it turned up that the pirates sieged us. Tis is messy but if you saw it your majesty you would not read my lines with your gracious smile. Cos when I saw the blood in the captain's cabin tat hit me so sensitively like two evenly big slaps. Or even deeper.

Finaly though this Dirty Alfred named (that's always stirring it and he keeps finding just me, on the Earth globe) invented a new type of hunting boat: He shot the water for them out of the barrel! Then followed the general public armed surrender.

A single old bearded scoundrel arrested about a hundred twenty pirates!

But he pitied them and did not escort them into any district police office.

Rear admiral Anderson sermon named round hearing was beautiful, memorable from my ruling time at your sirship, spectacular and boring. This handled us in order. And said that he would be happy to pin Busy Weesel (who wounded on the arm) and Butthead (whose snout was shredded) 1 medal.

But tis Dirt Alfred did not come!

Tis only interested in 3 things: money and nothing else and to play dirty on me. Until I also play dirty with one of his eyes. Even the blubeard appeared in the entrance hall and the cloakroomist helped the door off him. (Tis moron always drags everything along!)

By the way! It is good that I mentioned tis nitwit in my leter!

Cos in the end I gave it back to the Blubeard, I mean I took it back. Cos tis once put me in a tight spot when hired the Blind Dad so that I was forced to give him a third. Though he really does not deserve anything for his work. Unless I count that once from the guard tower he dropped the door onto the Copper Baron's head. He deserv some for this, but not a third. Otherwise he just drinks and sings and hugs everyone (Despite being hit on the head.) So I was happy that he gave back the third.

And even tis I can thank your majesty for!

Namely: A dated letter I declared to tell your Majesty that tis Bluebeard is, who is a famous and asked if Majesty knows him? In Frisco I received your loyal lines where your Majesty answers my question. And mentioned that heard of just 1 Bluebeard, but rather read.

Unfortunately I rarely get to a newspaper!

And Majesty wrote that this famous Bluebeard life story everyone could read. Even knows a musical opera performance of him.

This tallied! Cos this Wagner always comes with the opera that he's got something to do with! And your Majesty wrote that it was written of this Bluebeard that he was living in bigamist, with multiple wives, which the law punishes with strict hunt. And you wrote that this Bluebeard, if he no longer wanted one of the wives, did away with the mentioned, by means of murder. Your Majesty also wrote that this is likely not the same Bluebeard as the drunken named Wagner. But I tried it.

Your Majesty, everything matches! It's him!

There cannot be two men in the world with such blue beard. There also cannot be two such punches in the world that the Toungetied (about 8 feet) Trugitch gave this Wagner so he jumped head first into the enamel. I tried him in the Three-Mast Soda if it was him that your Majesty wrote about. I told him face to face, suddenly like this:

"You Wagner! Don't deny that you committed bigamism! You had more wives!"

Your Majesty! This was bullseye! The chap fell to his knees!

"Mercy!... My dear chum strovacheck! I thought nobody knew cos I was in Southamerica."

"See you moron! Cos accidentally Samtantonio high prince king found out about you and wrote me and it was in the papers as well that you are guilty of more than two marrying."

He admitted this but he claimed that he did without a name. So an even more fake one that he has now. And he went to Sweeden from Southamerica and only married third time after he arrived, but not from malice but money.

At this I snapped at him don't cry here because the bigamist belongs in prison and it is vileness that he deletes the wife he dislikes from the living. Well tis is where Your Majesty is wrong. Cos he claims, crying and swearing and still credibly that it was the opposite, because two of the previous wives nearly kill him and the scar on his forehead where his wife named Rita Amanda chucked a hot iron at him with intent to hurt. And he also said that if he killed the previous wives he would be innocent cos according to the bigamy law it is only forbidden to marry another woman if the previous wife is alive.

(This sounded very likely. If he kills the previous wives, he is innocent, because multiple marriage can't be done by a widow.)

He deserved it from me especially to blackmail him for recompensation because when I went for water (I was in disguise so that they believed I was a dead pirate), for that occasion this bluebeard hit me on the head. If I jump up and I hand him the slosh first, than today this will not argue with anybody. He though ran into the slosh twice with door an' all so it's no big deal that I was out.

I mention that the tourist on the André Deremio are not tourists. In secret they were looking for a mineral, which is called manganese ore. Of course in royal circles it would be called more elegant and wouldn't be named manganese ore but mineral ore. And there is a machine on the ship that makes water from sea the way that the salt is dusted off it by cooling it. It's called ventilator. So I am bold to assure your Majesty subjectly our graceful good will and I also remain;

Your Majesty's benevolent well-wisher:

Don Smiley di st. James

… Every sailor, who was in Frisco at the time, was very surprised that the Hountler returning from the hunt did not bring a single whale from the trip. Despite this, the crew did not complain.

Dirty Fred was different to a simple sailor. As the crew of the Hountler said to those who enquired, any fool can carry cargo and kill whales once they learned how to do it.

But the captain has all that brain!

Dirty Fred is the prime minister of the ocean. This is where he does his business! But, as the saving idea with the harpoon showed, his diplomacy is also worked when he engaged in barrel politics.

… More could have been said by Red Vasich perhaps, who (like the crew of the Hountler) had plenty of money. But Vasich only muttered a few words about the secretive case when he was dead drunk. Nobody understood that either:

"Everyone open… your eyes… wide…", he stammered as if giving some important lesson. "Then he will recognise, like a bird by its fountain feather… And that's where the bottom line of the dog is buried…"

Printed in Great Britain
by Amazon